## "W[...] com[...]ed to Emma
## over the phone

as she listened to the sound of rain beginning to come down on the roof of the house.
"I didn't know it was supposed to rain."

"Sam, it's perfectly nice out," Emma said.

"I can hear it raining," Sam challenged.

"That's weird," Emma said, "because I
can see the moon right from my bedroom
window."

"I guess it's one of those really local
storms or— Oh, my God!"

Sam slammed the phone down and took
off like a rocket up the stairs.

The slippery stairs. Which were covered
with water, with a pool at the landing.

It was too late. Far too late. When Sam
opened the door to the Flirts's bathroom, the
bath she'd been looking forward to having
had long since overflowed—there were at
least two inches of water, and another
inch of bubbles, on the bathroom floor.

Instantly, Sam turned off the water
going into the tub.

The silence was deafening . . .

# Sunset Fling

## CHERIE BENNETT

**Sunset™ Island**

**SPLASH™**

A BERKLEY / SPLASH BOOK

SUNSET FLING is an original publication of
The Berkley Publishing Group.
This work has never appeared before in book form.

SUNSET FLING

A Berkley Book / published by arrangement with
General Licensing Company, Inc.

PRINTING HISTORY
Berkley edition / July 1995

A GLC BOOK

*Splash* and *Sunset Island* are trademarks belonging to
General Licensing Company, Inc.

ISBN: 0-425-15026-7

BERKLEY®
Berkley Books are published by
The Berkley Publishing Group,
200 Madison Avenue, New York, New York 10016.
BERKLEY and the "B" design
are trademarks belonging to Berkley Publishing Corporation.

PRINTED IN THE UNITED STATES OF AMERICA

10  9  8  7  6  5  4  3  2  1

For my sweetie. Happy fifth anniversary!

# Sunset Fling

# ONE

"Gimme those binoculars!" Samantha Bridges yelled over the noisy whir of the helicopter. She grabbed the binoculars that were slung around her friend Emma Cresswell's neck.

"What for?" Emma asked, taking the binoculars off and handing them to Sam.

"Look!" Sam commanded, pointing excitedly toward the ground.

"I don't see anything," her other friend, Carrie Alden, shouted.

"Are you guys blind?" Sam cried as she squinted into the binoculars.

"What?" Emma asked again, as Sam pointed wildly.

1

"Look at that couple! Down on the beach! Near the far pier!"

"What about them?" Emma yelled. "I don't see anything!"

"They're doing it!" Sam shouted, her red hair flying crazily as she whipped her head around to look at her friends. "I can't believe it! Right on the beach!"

"That's so tacky," Emma said, wrinkling her perfect nose.

"It's probably Diana," Sam quipped, referring to Diana De Witt, the girls' arch-enemy. "She'd do it with anyone, anytime, anywhere."

Carrie and Emma cracked up.

Sam's boyfriend, Presley Travis, took the binoculars from Sam for a quick look. "I don't mean to break your heart," Pres drawled in his east Tennessee accent, "but your imagination is runnin' a little wild on you, girl."

"How so?" Sam asked.

"That dude is merely puttin' suntan lotion on his girlfriend's back," Pres said.

"You're sure?" Sam said, grabbing the binoculars back from Pres and peering through them again.

2

"Yep," Pres said.

"You're right," Sam replied, a little crest-fallen, as she took the binoculars away from her eyes.

"Coming up on the right is the main beach," the pilot announced, "and we'll soon be following Shore Road right around the island."

It was early Sunday morning on fabulous Sunset Island, the resort island off the coast of Maine at the far reaches of Casco Bay. And Pres, Sam, and her two best friends, Carrie and Emma, had decided to take advantage of one of the new tourist attractions on the island—a thirty-minute sightseeing helicopter ride. The four of them had met at the helipad at seven-thirty, as the tours were least expensive before eight in the morning.

"This is the coolest!" Sam shouted exuberantly. "The beach never looked so good. I've got to buy my own helicopter one of these days."

"With what money?" Carrie asked her.

"Hey, you know I'm going to be rich and famous," Sam declared.

"Of course," Emma teased. "You're going

3

to be a model-dancer-actress-singer, right? Oh, and I forgot—a fashion designer, too."

"Oh, I already am all of that," Sam said breezily. "I'll have to find something new to excel at." She turned to Carrie, whose face was looking white. "Hey, you okay?"

"Just great," Carrie maintained.

"Are you sure?" Emma asked with concern.

"I'll be a lot better when this ride is over," Carrie admitted.

"I think it's incredible!" Sam yelled again.

As the helicopter continued to fly two thousand feet above the island, Sam thought about how many great adventures she'd had since she'd been hired to work as an au pair for the Jacobs family here on Sunset Island.

*It's been an adventure,* she mused, *and it's not over yet!*

Sam thought back on the incredible circumstances that had brought her to the island, and then, even more incredibly, made her, Carrie Alden, and Emma Cresswell best friends.

They had all met two springs ago in New York City, when Sam and Emma were eighteen and Carrie was seventeen, at the International Au Pair Convention. Each of them was trying to line up a summer job in which they'd work for a family with children in exchange for room, board, and a small salary.

Then, they'd all been hired by families who had summer houses on Sunset Island— their first choice and just about the most coveted location offered at the convention. They'd spent the previous summer working for their respective employers and had been invited back for a second summer.

*I'd change families if I could,* Sam thought. *Sometimes Dan Jacobs and his fourteen-year-old twin girls are a bit much for anyone to handle. But Emma and Carrie are the best friends any girl could ever want.*

*Not that I would have expected to be friends with them, let alone even have met them! Emma is a perfect blonde with a perfect figure from a perfect Boston family with a ton of money, even if her mother is at the moment in the process of cutting her off from it. And Carrie? Your basic brunette-next-door-with-brains from New Jersey who thinks she's a little too curvy and is a student at Yale planning to be a photojournalist. Who'd think they'd be friends with me, the tall redheaded dance fiend from the booming metropolis of Junction, Kansas . . . where there are probably more pigs and cows than people?*

*And Pres,* Sam thought. *Who would have thought that a guy as cute and cool as he is would—*

"There's Kurt's house!" Emma yelled, pointing down as the helicopter passed over the island's weathered commercial fishing and lobstering harbor. Tourism had replaced fishing as the key industry on Sunset Island, but the lobster boats still set out on their morning rounds every day, and the party fishing boats anchored in the harbor went out with their day's fares.

"I think you're right," Carrie said, looking out the window. "I'm sure that's it."

"And there's Kurt!" Emma cried. She waved frantically at the tall, brown-haired guy she could just make out behind the house, but he didn't take any notice of the helicopter.

Kurt Ackerman was the guy Emma had

met her first summer on Sunset Island. They had fallen totally in love. Kurt had been raised on the island and knew all the locals. He was from a poor family and Emma from a rich one, and their romance didn't seem to make anyone in either family happy except Emma and Kurt.

*They've had some big ups and downs,* Sam mused. *The big wedding, for example. Or should I say the big almost-wedding?*

"We're landing now," the pilot called back over the intercom. "Sit tight!"

The helicopter was now poised over an open field. Sam looked out. They were five hundred feet up. In the middle of the field was a big red circular target.

*That's our landing pad,* she thought.

"Hey," she joked, "think if I jump now I could make a bull's-eye?"

"With *your* head," Pres drawled, "you'd likely make a hole in the ground twenty feet deep."

"Thanks, big guy," Sam said with a laugh.

A minute later, they were on the ground. The pilot, a short, balding man wearing coveralls, turned to them. "So, was it worth it to get up so early?" he asked.

7

"Absolutely," Carrie assured him. She patted her photographic gear, which was slung around her neck. "I got some great shots—even if I did feel a little queasy there for a while."

"Hey, look for those photos in the *Breakers* next week," Sam told the pilot. The *Breakers* was the island's weekly newspaper, and Carrie did occasional freelance work for it.

"I didn't make a deal to sell these to the *Breakers*," Carrie said, turning to Sam.

"Not yet," Sam assured her. "Not yet." Then she glanced at her watch. Eight o'clock. "Yo, let's get this show on the road. I'm late."

"Sure," Carrie joked. "What'll happen if you're late? Dan'll fire you?"

"Put you out on the street?" Emma suggested, joining in the fun.

"No way," Sam replied, tying her windblown hair back into a ponytail.

"You sure?" Pres asked her.

"Sure I'm sure," Sam maintained. "Because no one else would ever take the job! And take care of the twin monsters? I don't think so!"

*　　*　　*

Emma dropped Sam off at the Jacobses' house at ten minutes after eight.

*Early!* Sam thought triumphantly as she let herself in. *I had to be back by 8:15. I hope it's not too much of a zoo in there. Dixie Mason spent the night again with the twins.*

"Hey, gang," Sam yelled as she came through the front hallway and into the kitchen, where Dan Jacobs, Allie and Becky—Sam could tell the twins apart only because Becky had a small mole right above her lip—and their friend Dixie were eating breakfast. "You guys find the breakfast stuff okay?"

The three girls looked up at her. Dan Jacobs's head was buried in the Sunday *Portland Press-Herald.* He was dressed in his typical golf outfit: plaid trousers and a lime-green golf shirt—and Sam remembered he had a standing golf foursome on Sundays.

*Serious fashion risk,* Sam thought, wincing at the colorful outfit.

"Sure," Allie Jacobs said. "No thanks to you, though."

9

"What are you talking about?" Sam said as she poured a cup of coffee and pulled up a chair at the table.

"Sam," Becky said, as if she were talking to a six-year-old, "you know we hate granola."

"Hate it," Allie echoed.

"Wait a sec," Sam protested. "Last week you guys told me you loved granola."

"Not with raisins in it," Becky said, making a face. "Raisins are so disgusting." She held her bowl of cereal out to Sam. "Tell me that doesn't look like a zillion dead cockroaches doing the dead man's float in that milk."

"So take the raisins out," Sam said with exaggerated patience.

Allie sighed dramatically and poured herself a glass of juice. "Somehow I've lost my appetite."

"How was the helicopter ride, Sam?" Dan said, finally looking up from his newspaper. "Lots of people on the golf course yet?"

"Not that I could see," Sam replied, taking a sip of her coffee.

*I can't believe he lets the twins get away*

*with the way they act toward me some-
times,* Sam thought. *They get away with
murder, and he lets them.* She turned to
Dixie Mason, who hadn't opened her mouth
yet, and smiled. "So, how are you doing this
morning, Dix?"

"Just fine," Dixie drawled, "and I like
granola."

Dixie had been born and raised in Mississippi, where her parents were both pro-
fessors at Mississippi State University in
tiny Starkville. Along with Becky and Allie, she was a counselor-in-training at the
country club day camp.

"Thanks, Dix," Sam said, taking one of
the cinnamon rolls left on the table. "It's
nice to know someone appreciates me."

"Oh, I do," Dixie said solemnly. Dixie was
really smart in addition to being really
pretty—she'd been America's Little Miss
Sweetheart when she was seven, and had
even helped coach Sam when Sam entered
the Miss Sunset Island contest earlier in
the summer.

"Granola's great if there's ice on your
driveway," Dixie continued. "It snowed last

11

January in Starkville, and Mom threw granola on our driveway. No one fell."

The twins cracked up. Even Dan Jacobs smiled from behind his newspaper.

"You guys have camp today, right?" Sam asked.

"Duh," Allie said.

"Double duh," Becky echoed.

"Triple duh," Dixie contributed.

"Dixie," Sam said, "you are hanging around Becky and Allie too much. They're rubbing off on you."

"I hope so!" Dixie said, her eyes lighting up. "Because my life used to be sooooo boring!" She threw her arms around Becky and Allie, who were sitting on either side of her, and pulled them to her. Their faces close together, the three girls smiled beatifically.

"You want me to baby-sit tonight, Dan?" Sam asked her boss.

"That'd be great, Sam," Dan said, "because I've got a date—"

"Puh-leeze," Becky interrupted her dad, "we do not need Sam to baby-sit!"

"We're fourteen," Allie echoed.

"Sam is staying," Dan said, his voice a little stern. "Kiki and I—"

"We don't need her, Dad," Becky implored. "We're old enough to take care of ourselves."

Dan sighed. "I'll make that decision," he said. "Sam, I'll need you tonight until ten, all right? After that, you're free."

"Cool," Sam said. She was going to meet Emma and Carrie at the Play Café when she got off work, no matter how late that was.

"Another boring evening," Becky grumbled.

"Prisoners in our own home," Allie added.

"Life sucks, then you die," Sam quipped over her coffee. *I don't care what kind of mood the twins are in,* she thought. *I will not let them get to me today. I'm going to go out tonight after Dan gets home, and I'm going to have a blast.*

"Maybe we could go out with you," Becky asked Sam hopefully. "The Play Café, maybe?"

"Nope," Sam said. "But I will rent you guys a movie. How's that?"

"Oh, great," Allie said, her voice dripping

13

with sarcasm. "Just make sure that it's X-rated."

"Y'all get to watch X-rated movies?" Dixie asked hopefully.

"Not in this lifetime," Dan said with a smile.

"Oh, that's just great," Allie said, pushing herself out of her chair. "One of these days Becky and I are going to declare our independence, you know."

"That's right," Becky agreed, standing up next to her sister. "And when we do, watch out!"

"Why, what would happen?" Dixie asked her friends.

"Whatever we want to have happen," Allie said. "And when that day comes, no one and nothing is going to stop us!"

# TWO

*At last,* Sam thought when she heard the front door open and then close again. *Dan's finally home. He's a half-hour late. If he were working for me, I'd fire him!*

Sam got up from her bed, where she'd been waiting for Dan Jacobs to come home from his date. Becky and Allie were watching a video in Becky's room. She took one last look at herself in the mirror, and smiled at herself approvingly.

"Sam Bridges," she said out loud to herself, "you are an awesome fox."

For her night at the Play Café with Carrie and Emma, Sam had chosen a tiny, white stretchy T-shirt that bared her navel, and a full cotton miniskirt with a drawstring waist that hit her right at the hipbone. On her feet were her trademark red cowboy boots.

"You are almost too cute to live," she told her reflection. Then she winked at herself once more in the mirror, and zipped down-stairs.

"Hey, Sam," Dan said as Sam started to rush by him, "you look nice."

"Thanks. I hope you had fun tonight."

"It was great!" Dan said heartily. "Thanks for asking!"

*What's he so exuberant about?* Sam won-dered. *I was only trying to be the dutiful employee. Well, whatever. I never have un-derstood the guy.* "Okay," Sam said, "I'm outta here."

"Uh, Sam?" Dan asked, sounding ner-vous.

Sam stopped in her tracks. "Yes?" she asked.

"Can I talk to you about something?"

"Sure," Sam said, trying not to feel an-noyed that he was holding up her plans to leave.

"I think we should go in the kitchen,"

Dan said quickly, and turned in that direction. Sam had no choice but to follow him there.

*Damn,* Sam thought. *I hope it isn't over that stupid granola incident this morning. Because his darling little twins were completely, totally, and indescribably obnoxious to me. But if that's it, why didn't he talk to me about it before he went out on his date? There was plenty of time.*

Dan pulled a chair out from the kitchen table and sat down. So did Sam.

"So," Dan said.

"So," Sam echoed.

"Uh, can I get you some water?" Dan asked.

"Sure," Sam replied, totally puzzled. "Whatever."

Dan got up and got two water glasses out of the cupboard. Then he got the bottle of spring water out of the fridge and brought it to the table. He poured himself a glass, and a glass for Sam.

"Thanks," Sam said, fighting an urge to check her watch. *I know Carrie and Emma are already at the Play Café waiting for me,*

17

she thought impatiently. *And I'm sitting here drinking spring water with Dan. Great.*

"Sam," Dan began, "you know I think you've done a wonderful job with the girls."

"Well, I try."

"They like you so much!" Dan said earnestly. "You're like an older sister to them."

"I appreciate that," Sam replied.

*Older sister?* Sam thought. *Please. My little sister, Ruth Ann, is absolutely nothing like the twins. If she tried to get away with what they do, my parents would kill her first and ask questions later.*

Dan took a sip of water. "It's such a shame their mother couldn't see them now."

Sam was silent. What could she say? The twins' mother had walked out on the family years earlier, and no one knew where she was.

"They look up to you," Dan continued, staring at his glass of water.

"I like them," Sam said honestly. "They're basically good kids." What she wanted to add, but didn't, was that they were basically good kids with basically rotten attitudes.

"I think they're immature," Dan said

18

flatly. "Like that granola thing this morning. That was obnoxious."

"I'm glad you agree," Sam said, looking at her watch pointedly. She really was not anxious to get into a protracted discussion with Dan Jacobs over the psychological problems of his two daughters, even if she was sort of shocked that Dan was paying any attention to those problems at all.

"Well," Dan said, his eyes fixed on the table, "Kiki and I have been talking."

"Yes?" Sam prompted, a little hesitantly. Kiki Coors was the actress whom Dan had been dating recently.

*Of course, the only reason they even met is that Becky and Allie hired Kiki to pose as a glamorous version of their mother at Club Sunset Island's Parents' Day. That's where Dan met her for the first time. And now they're dating! Why, Kiki actually bosses the twins around like she is their mother now,* Sam recalled.

"Kiki thinks they need to grow up," Dan said.

"It wouldn't hurt," Sam agreed. "She's right about that."

"She thinks they need more responsibility," Dan related.

Sam nodded.

"And she thinks they need to learn to act like adults," Dan continued.

*Great,* Sam thought. *Now I know everything that Kiki thinks. Like I care what Kiki thinks about anything. What does Dan think?*

"I agree with Kiki," Dan said, answering her thought.

*What a shocker,* Sam thought, taking another little peek at her watch. *Now he's probably going to ask me to spend even more time with them, to be even more of a role model and a good influence. This must be my lucky day.*

"So," Sam finally said, "that's all really good, I think. And if there's anything I can do to help—"

"There is," Dan said, looking up at her.

"Just tell me," Sam said brightly. *And tell me quick so I can leave,* she added in her mind.

"The thing is, Sam," Dan began slowly, "Kiki thinks . . . well, Kiki thinks that the girls don't need an au pair anymore."

20

"She *what?*" Sam asked, stunned.

"She thinks the girls would be better off without an au pair," Dan repeated. "She thinks it would force them to take some responsibility around here."

"Uh-huh," Sam mumbled, thinking this was the craziest thing she'd ever heard.

"She thinks they'll look after themselves," Dan continued.

"Uh-huh."

"And grow up faster."

"You don't agree with her, do you?" Sam asked, astonished by the conversation she was having. "Because if you do, why don't you have Kiki come in and take care of your daughters for—"

"I think I do agree with her," Dan replied.

"So what's going on? You're *firing* me?" Sam asked.

"No, no, not at all!" Dan assured her. "My girls have just outgrown their need for an au pair. You've been wonderful, Sam."

"But you just told me they would be better off without me," Sam pointed out. "That's firing!"

"That's just semantics," Dan said, wav-

21

ing his hand in the air. "You had to know that your job here wouldn't last forever."

"I am completely confused," Sam said. "Are you firing me or aren't you firing me?"

"I wouldn't call it firing you," Dan said with a frown. "I mean, that implies that I'm unhappy with your performance. . . ."

"What do you call it, then?" Sam exclaimed, her hands trembling.

"Restructuring our arrangement," Dan decided, but he couldn't quite meet Sam's eyes.

"I don't believe this!" Sam cried. "I really don't believe this!" Then a thought occurred to her. "Wait, you can't fire me! It's in the contract from the au pair agency. You hired me for the whole summer!"

Dan shook his head. "Kiki and I went over your agreement. I can let you go. I just can't kick you out of here. Not that I ever would, Sam. We consider you practically a member of the family—"

"Really?" Sam's voice was bitter. "Then you must not treat your family very well."

"Look, I know this is sudden," Dan said gently, "but I have to do what I think is best for my girls. I'm sure you understand that."

"No, I really don't," Sam said. "I've put up with a lot from them. I've done everything you've ever asked me to do. You tell me what a great influence I've been on them, and then you kick me out."

"I'm not kicking you out," Dan said quickly. "According to your contract, I have to offer you housing—at a market-rate rent," he went on. He pulled a piece of paper out of his pocket and began to read. Sam could see that it was the simple agreement Dan had signed with the International Au Pair Society when Sam had originally been hired.

"Clause twelve," Dan read. "'Employer may discharge employee at any time for cause. If discharge is not due to employee's conduct or performance, employer must offer employee housing through the summer, in her original quarters, at the market rate.'"

"Hold on," Sam said. "Are you telling me that I can live here but I don't have a job and you're going to *charge me rent?*"

"The contract says—"

"How am I supposed to pay rent?" Sam practically screamed. "I don't have a job anymore!"

"Kiki and I talked it over, and I've decided not to charge you rent for the rest of the summer," Dan said, looking uncomfortable.

"But I won't have any income," Sam said. "I can't even eat."

"I'm sure you'll find another job," Dan said. "You'll have two whole weeks. I have to give you that much notice. And a free place to live isn't nothing, you know. A room like that would rent for a lot of money."

"Oh, so am I supposed to *thank* you?" Sam asked incredulously.

"Look, Sam, I'm sorry, but circumstances change. It's just time for us to move on. . . ."

"Move on," Sam echoed dully.

"Right," Dan said. "You'll still get to see the girls, of course. I don't think suddenly whisking you out of their lives would be a good thing for them. But now you can be a friend who lives here, and the twins will

24

have to take more responsibility for their lives."

Sam stood up angrily. "You know, Mr. Jacobs, you are really a coward. You're firing me, plain and simple. You just don't want to use those words because you want to think of yourself as such a nice guy."

"That's not fair—"

"You're the one who's not being fair," Sam shot back, so angry that tears came to her eyes. "And you don't have to worry about firing me, because I quit."

"Sam, don't be like that—"

"Just give me those two weeks to find another job," Sam snapped, "and I am out of your life forever."


Sam spotted Emma and Carrie as soon as she walked into the Play Café. The two of them were sitting together in their usual booth, under one of the Play Café's many rock-video monitors.

As usual, Sam had to squeeze through the crowd to get to her friends, and as usual, she saw eight or ten people she knew on the way to the table. She even ran into Darcy Laken, who was in the café with her friend Scott, an officer on the island's tiny police force.

Finally she got to the table where Emma and Carrie were sharing a pitcher of iced tea and sat down.

"How are the monsters?" Emma joked as Sam slid into the booth.

"Dead," Sam replied flatly.

Carrie laughed. "That bad, huh? They kept you working late?"

"Worse," Sam responded, pouring herself a tall glass of iced tea.

"Impossible," Carrie said. "Nothing is worse than the monsters."

"How about getting fired by the monsters' father?" Sam asked, taking a sip from her glass.

"What?" Emma asked.

"Nice joke, Sam." Carrie grinned.

"No joke," Sam said. "I'm telling you, Dan Jacobs just fired me!"

"Come on," Emma prompted, "cut it out."

"I'm totally serious." Sam put her head down on the table. "I am so screwed."

"What happened?" Emma demanded.

"Some huge disaster?" Carrie asked.

"That's just the thing," Sam said, feeling

furious all over again. "I didn't do anything wrong! Dan even said so!"

Sam then told her friends the story of her conversation with Dan. When she got to the part about Kiki Coors and how Dan had talked the whole thing over with her, both Emma and Carrie sat back in the booth, speechless.

"The worst part is," Sam summed up, "there's not a thing I can do about it."

"Wow," Carrie breathed. "I don't know what to say. It's terrible!"

"Maybe you could try talking to Kiki?" Emma ventured.

"I doubt it," Sam said. "Now that I think about it, she's been dropping all these hints, you know? About how the girls don't need a baby-sitter anymore."

"Maybe you could try reasoning with Dan again," Carrie suggested. "After all, he and Kiki aren't even engaged or anything."

"It doesn't matter," Sam said. "Dan thinks Kiki is the Second Coming."

"He worships her," Carrie agreed.

"Oh, man, I can't believe this is happening," Sam groaned.

Emma picked up one of the nachos they'd ordered in advance of Sam's arrival and bit off the tip of it thoughtfully. "What are you going to do?" she asked Sam.

"I'm not certain," Sam said truthfully. "I'm not certain at all. But two things are for sure."

"What's that?" Carrie asked, raising her voice as the music in the café got louder.

"One, I'm not going back to Kansas unless I'm in a pine box," Sam declared.

Her friends laughed.

"*I* am allowed to laugh at Kansas," Sam commented dryly. "*You* may not. And two, I'm never going to work for fourteen-year-old twins ever again."

"But what are you going to do?" Emma asked.

Sam sighed. "Got me. I can't even beg you to support me in a style to which I would like to become accustomed, now that your mother has cut off the gravy train."

"Please, don't bring up my mother," Emma said, shaking her head.

"Seriously, Sam," Carrie said. "Do you have a plan?"

"No," Sam admitted. "Dan just hit me

with this bombshell." She took a long drink of her iced tea. "Look, I've got two weeks if I need it. And this isn't Siberia. I just want to get out of there as soon as I can."

"Meaning?" Carrie prompted.

"Meaning I'll find myself a job, and I'll find another place to live," Sam said emphatically, picking up a couple of nachos and stuffing them in her mouth.

"Good for you," Emma said, a note of admiration in her voice.

"Maybe you'll sell more Samstyles," Carrie offered hopefully.

"That'd be nice," Sam said. "But they're not exactly flying out of the Cheap Boutique."

Samstyles was a line of clothing that the Cheap Boutique had asked Sam to put together for them—more like one-of-a-kinds than anything else. They were outfits held together not by thread and seams, but by safety pins and costume-jewelry brooches. Sam had entered one in a design contest the boutique had sponsored, and it had come in second.

"You've sold a couple," Emma pointed out.

"A couple won't make me rich," Sam sighed. "Besides, I blew that money on more material so I could make more Sam-styles."

"In other words, you're broke," Carrie said.

"Something like that," Sam admitted.

"I'd ask you to help us with the per-fume," Emma said softly, "but we're not turning enough of a profit yet to need help."

The perfume was Sunset Magic, which Carrie and Emma had put together with the father of their good friend, Erin Kane. Emma had financed the whole thing—and now that she was having money problems with her mother, the whole venture was in jeopardy.

Erin's dad had assured them that he wouldn't let Sunset Magic go belly up, but he was having so many problems of his own as a result of the recent stock market decline that it was hard for any of the girls to actually believe him.

Carrie nodded. "Everyone loves the per-fume. That's not the problem. But because we made the whole thing with natural ingredients, it costs us more to manufacture it."

"We need a higher profit margin without compromising the product," Emma explained.

Sam looked at her blankly.

"Forget it," Emma said. "We weren't talking about our perfume business, we were talking about you."

"Well, no matter what happens," Sam decided, "I'm going to live like a real human being. No kids to look after—I'll be in heaven."

"What kind of job do you think you'll look for?" Carrie asked, reaching for a nacho.

Sam shrugged. "I'll find something."

"It's not so easy on this island in the middle of the season," Carrie reminded her.

"Hey, I'm resourceful," Sam said. "Maybe I could be Pres's love slave."

"Does that pay very well?" Emma asked with a smile.

"I don't know. I'll have to look into it," Sam replied. She looked around the café without really seeing it. "Anyway, I got this job with the Jacobses, so surely I can find another one."

"I'm sure you will," Emma told her, clearly trying her best to sound supportive.

"Me, too," Carrie added.

*Right,* Sam said to herself. *I have to find a job. I just have to. Because if I don't, it's good-bye, Sunset Island.*

# THREE

*Beep, beep! Beep, beep! Beep, beep!*

Sam sleepily reached for the small alarm clock that was perched on the nightstand next to her bed and snapped it off with a sharp whack of her fist.

*Eight o'clock in the morning,* she thought as she pulled herself out of a deep sleep. *I always wake up at eight o'clock in the morning. Got to get breakfast together for the monsters.*

She swung her legs out of her bed and reached for an old sweatshirt to pull on over the Kansas State University T-shirt she slept in.

And then it hit her.

33

She wasn't working for Dan Jacobs anymore. She'd lost her job the night before. Correction: She'd been fired the night before. Or she'd quit. Or both.

*No breakfast today for the monsters,* Sam thought. *No breakfast tomorrow for the monsters. No breakfast ever again for the monsters. Because I don't work for the monsters anymore!*

She sat on the edge of her bed, feeling stunned.

*I don't have to be downstairs for breakfast at any certain hour,* she thought. *And I don't ever have to hear again about how disgusting granola is! That's good. However, I'm unemployed and broke. That's bad.*

She stood up and stretched. "Well, I might as well get up and go eat," she said out loud. "And start to look for a job."

*I know, I'll scan the paper,* she thought as she brushed her teeth. *I'll find a job. I'll definitely find a job.*

She dressed quickly in a pair of jeans and a fresh T-shirt and went downstairs, where Becky and Allie were already sitting at the kitchen table, talking quietly.

The talk stopped as soon as Sam came into the kitchen; the room was totally quiet, except for the sound of the twins spooning cereal into their mouths. It was the same granola with raisins they'd made such a fuss about the day before.

Sam walked over to the coffee machine and poured herself a cupful.

"You're eating granola," she said, staring at Becky.

"Yum, granola!" Becky exclaimed. "I just totally love fresh granola, don't you, Allie?"

"Can't get enough of it!" Allie replied, digging in with her spoon and taking a big mouthful.

"It's the best!" Becky commented.

"Better than that!" Allie quipped.

"Uh," Sam put in, interrupting the granola rhapsody, "excuse me, guys, but can I ask what's going on here?"

"Breakfast!" Becky replied, holding up a big spoonful of the cereal.

"We love it!" Allie piped up. "Granola!"

"Food of the gods," Becky stated. "Can you pass me some more?"

As Becky stuck her arm out to reach for the box of cereal, Sam noticed something really strange—Becky was wearing a home-made black armband around the left sleeve of her bright blue Club Sunset Island sweat-shirt. She glanced quickly over at Allie. Same armband.

"What's with the armbands?" Sam asked, picking up a muffin that was on a plate on the table.

"Protesting," Becky said, spooning up her cereal.

"Demonstrating," Allie chimed in.

"Voting with our clothes," Becky added.

"Dad told us that Kiki said you had to be fired," Becky said.

"We think it sucks," Allie opined.

"Kiki's a lamebrain," Becky told Sam matter-of-factly. "I don't know why he listens to her."

"Because she has big—you know," Allie replied.

"So what?" Becky asked. "That doesn't mean she has a brain to call her own."

"That's for sure," Allie scoffed.

"So we're protesting," Becky added.

"That's why we're wearing armbands," Allie said.

"It was my idea," Becky said proudly.

36

"No, it wasn't," Allie retorted.

"Was."

"Wasn't!"

"Okay! Okay! It doesn't matter whose idea it was! Where is your father?" Sam asked. She bit into her muffin.

"Guess," Allie said, rolling her eyes. "Two points, you're right. Upstairs."

"And guess who he's with," Becky added, making a nasty face.

"When did she come over?" Sam asked, realizing that Kiki hadn't come home with Dan the night before.

"About midnight," Becky answered. "We heard her come in the back door."

"It's all your fault!" Allie said to Becky accusingly, pointing her finger at her twin sister.

"Is not!" Becky shot back.

"Is!" Allie said. "You're the one who first brought her into this house!"

"I had no choice!" Becky answered, her voice rising an octave, "because—"

"All right, all right," Sam said, cutting Becky off. "No use crying over spilled milk. It's over now."

"So are you," Allie said sadly.

"It's all our fault," Becky agreed, her voice matching Allie's tone.

"We blew it," Allie said.

"That's true," Sam said lightly. "You guys did blow it." And then she thought of something. "When did your father tell you I was outta here?" she continued. "Because I talked to him late last night, and—"

"About fifteen minutes ago," Becky interrupted Sam. "He came down to make some coffee to bring upstairs to . . . well, you know."

"We tried to talk him out of it," Allie said hotly. "But it was no deal."

"He never listens to us," Becky said.

"He only listens to Kiki," Allie commented.

"The lamebrain," Becky snorted. "And he only likes her because of her gigunda—"

"Yeah, yeah, I heard that already," Sam reminded her.

"Anyway," Allie continued, "we tried to convince him that he should just apologize to you and say you should stay here."

"You know, plead temporary insanity," Becky added quickly.

"Even if we know better," Allie said significantly.

"But Dad said his mind was made up," Becky said, dropping her spoon in her bowl with a clatter. "And that he wasn't gonna change it."

"Dumb," Allie said. "Because he's sure not going to want to do your job."

"And neither is Kiki," Becky added. "Who's going to do the food shopping, and the cleaning up, and all that stuff? Not *moi*."

"Not *moi*, either," Allie added. "Some new person, I suppose."

"See, you love me because I'm your maid," Sam said. "Well, I used to be. Anyway, from what your dad said to me, you're not getting another au pair. It's just going to be your dad . . . and Kiki."

"Aaaargh!" Allie cried, reaching for her throat and falling to the ground.

Becky made fake gagging noises. "Not her!"

"I'd rather eat worms than have to listen to Kiki," Allie said from where she lay on the floor.

"Maggots," Becky said.

"Worms *and* maggots." Allie shuddered. "She'd probably make us dress like her, too. Gawd, I refuse to be seen in a leopard-print catsuit!"

Sam laughed. "You guys may be impossible," she told them, "but you are hilarious."

"To know us is to love us," Allie declared, using one of Sam's favorite phrases.

"Anyway," Becky said, "if you see the house burning down next week, you'll know we couldn't stand it even another minute."

"What are you gonna do?" Allie asked.

Sam shrugged. "I'm not sure," she said honestly. "Find another place to live. Get a job."

"You could live here!" Becky suggested.

"Yeah," Allie agreed. "Dad told us he told you that you could!"

"It would be so cool," Becky opined.

"We'd make you breakfast," Allie offered.

"Granola every day."

"And black coffee," Allie added.

"We'd have it waiting for you when you got up," Becky said.

Sam shook her head. "I don't think so," she said. "I'm going to find a place of my own."

Allie and Becky visibly sagged in their seats.

"Told you," Becky said to Allie.

"Yeah, but . . ." Allie's voice trailed off.

*They're actually disappointed that I'm not going to be here,* Sam realized. *They're actually going to miss me! They actually wish I could stay!* She asked the twins, "If you want me so much now, why did you always give me such a hard time when I was your au pair?"

"We're fourteen," Becky said simply. "We're *supposed* to give you a hard time."

"Hey," Allie said, "I just thought of something." She pushed her bowl of granola away from the edge of the table.

"Forget it," Becky said. "We don't earn enough to hire her ourselves."

"That wasn't it," Allie replied earnestly, then she turned to Sam. "Anyway, I think this is your big chance," she said, her brown eyes shining.

"What big chance?" Sam asked blankly, glancing at her watch. "Hey, the bus for camp comes in three minutes. You'll be late."

41

"You're not our au pair anymore," Becky said quickly. "If we're late, it's Dad's fault."

"And I don't see him anywhere," Allie added, taking a quick look around the kitchen. She settled back comfortably in her chair.

"What big chance?" Sam asked again, reminding Allie of what she'd said before.

"Oh!" Allie said. "I was just thinking . . ."

"Yes?" Sam prompted.

"Well, you need a place to live, right?"

"Yes," Sam replied, wondering where this was going.

"And you have a boyfriend, right?" Allie asked.

"Pres is so buff," Becky said, nodding. "If he ever gets tired of someone *old* like you—"

"Why don't you live with him?" Allie asked.

"Go for it, girlfriend!" Becky encouraged.

"Yeah!" Allie hooted.

"I don't know . . ." Sam began.

"Come on, it'd be so cool!" Becky cried. "How could you turn down a chance to live with Presley Travis, who is only the finest thing on two feet?"

42

"A lot of relationships get ruined when people live together," Sam said.

"But it would be so romantic!" Allie insisted. "Just you and him."

"And the entire band," Sam reminded her. "Besides, Pres and I aren't . . . uh . . ." *I was going to tell her that we aren't sleeping together, but maybe that's not such a good idea,* Sam thought.

"Doing the horizontal hoochie?" Becky asked. "For real?"

"How can you not be sleeping with him?" Allie asked in amazement. "We thought for sure you were!"

"Well, you thought wrong," Sam said. "Not that it's any of your business." She looked into her coffee cup and thought a moment. *Maybe it's not such a terrible idea, though, even if we aren't sleeping together yet,* she realized. *There's plenty of room in the Flirts's house. I know Pres and Billy did an acoustic gig last night in New Hampshire and won't be back until tomorrow . . . but maybe this is not a bad idea at all.*

The camp bus beeped its horn in the street outside the Jacobses' house.

"Gotta motor!" Allie said, jumping up from the table.

"See you later, Sam, we hope!" Becky said fervently.

"But if you're not here," Allie quipped as she headed for the door, "we'll look for you at Pres's house!"

"Did you really lose your job?" Ian Templeton asked Sam, walking over to her.

"Yep," Sam said, without picking her head up from the *Press-Herald*.

"Wow, man," Ian said seriously. "Tough break."

"Thanks, Ian," Sam said, a little patronizingly, looking up at Ian. "I appreciate your concern."

It was Monday afternoon, and Carrie had invited both Sam and Emma over to hang out by the pool at Graham Perry Templeton's house, where she worked as the au pair for his thirteen-year-old son, Ian, and five-year-old daughter, Chloe. Ian didn't go to Club Sunset Island, which was why he was hanging out by the pool.

Sam grinned when she saw Ian's outfit. He was wearing black combat boots, black jeans, a black sleeveless T-shirt that read *The Who: Live at Leeds,* and black wrap-around sunglasses. Ian had his own band, called Lord Whitehead and the Zit People, for which Becky and Allie Jacobs were backup singers.

*But he seems to be taking the rock-and-roll thing just a little bit too far now,* Sam thought.

"Didn't know you were into The Who," Sam commented, taking in Ian's outfit.

"Classic rock. They ruled," Ian stated seriously. "Right up there with my dad."

Ian's father was the rock legend everyone knew as Graham Perry, who'd grown up playing clubs on the Jersey shore and then made six or seven CDs that immediately went platinum, and whom people were already talking about for the Rock and Roll Hall of Fame.

*Carrie gets to work for Graham Perry,* Sam thought, *and I get to work for Dan Jacobs. Whoa. Reality check! I* used *to work for Dan Jacobs.*

"Of course," Ian went on, "the Zits are gonna be bigger than The Who ever was."

"Right," Sam said, looking back down at

the paper. The fact was, the Zits was one of the most atrocious bands that Sam had ever heard.

Emma climbed out of the pool and headed over to Sam. "Find anything?" she asked, toweling herself off as she walked.

"Not much," Sam admitted. "A few things that—"

The phone rang.

"I've got it," Carrie called. She got up from her lounge and went over to pick up the cordless phone. She seemed to be listening for a long time.

"Everything okay?" Sam said.

Carrie gave the thumbs-up sign, and then put her hand over the receiver.

"It's Darcy Laken!" she told them. "She said that she and Scott the cop just broke up, that she's met the most incredible guy, and that we have to meet him! She's going to marry him!"

"She's going to marry some guy she just met?" Sam asked incredulously.

"That doesn't sound like Darcy!" Emma exclaimed.

Darcy Laken was a very cool, very athletic, very tough girl who the girls had befriended that summer. She took care of Molly Mason, Dixie's cousin, a sixteen-year-old paraplegic who lived with her parents in a spooky house on the highest hill on the island.

"Darcy says the Masons' house, six-thirty tonight. You guys up for it? Dress formal!"

Emma nodded.

"A free meal?" Sam cried. "And I'm unemployed? Count me in!"

Carrie spoke to Darcy for another couple of minutes, then hung up and padded over to the other two girls. "This guy must really be something, huh?"

"And why would she want us to dress formally just to have dinner at her house?" Emma wondered, reaching for the suntan lotion.

"Maybe he's some rich oil sheik," Sam said, "and, like, he only wears tuxes. Maybe he'll hire me for a zillion dollars to dance in a show he's backing."

"And maybe you've been out in the sun too long," Carrie told her.

"And maybe you'd better find a job," Emma added, pointing at the want ads in the paper.

47

Sam sighed. There was hardly anything in the paper. Carrie was right. Jobs were not easy to find on Sunset Island.

Not easy at all.

# FOUR

"You have to admit, this place is mondo bizarro," Sam said as Emma pulled the Hewitts' car up to Molly Mason's house that evening.

"It's make-believe," Emma said, turning off the engine.

"I know that," Sam said. "But what kind of insane person decides to decorate their home like a haunted house? Answer me that."

"The kind who writes horror movies," Carrie said as the three of them walked toward the mansion.

Sam looked down at herself. "I feel kinda dumb all dressed up like this just to eat dinner at a friend's house." She had on a short black crepe dress with sheer sleeves—conservative for her—that she'd found at a secondhand store. Carrie had on wide-legged navy pants with a white silk blouse and a blue and white paisley vest, and Emma wore a new white lace minidress that her dad had recently sent her as a gift.

"It's a special dinner," Emma reminded her. "Supposedly Darcy is going to marry this guy."

"The only problem," Sam quipped, "is that I might be lookin' too good."

"What do you mean?" Carrie asked as the three of them walked up the long, long path to the huge front door of the Masons' house.

"Darcy's new guy's gonna fall in love with me!" Sam joked.

As they approached the house Sam looked up and took it all in. The house itself looked like something out of a gothic horror novel, with weather-beaten black shutters around an odd assortment of windows.

"Seriously warped," Sam said, still staring up at the house.

"Seriously," Carrie agreed.

"I remember the first time I came here," Emma said. "It was with Katie Hewitt."

"That was when you were collecting money for COPE, right?" Carrie asked. COPE was Citizens of Positive Ethics, a political and environmental group in which Kurt Ackerman, Emma's boyfriend, was really active, and for which all the girls had occasionally done volunteer work.

"Right," Emma replied. "She thought we were both going to die."

"So did you," Carrie joked.

*I thought the same thing, too, the first time I was here,* Sam recalled. *Because this house really is like something out of* The Bride of Frankenstein. *Not that it shouldn't be. Molly's parents write horror and slasher movies for a living, and they've decorated the house to match their jobs!*

"Hey," Sam said as they neared the ten-foot-high front door, which featured a knocker in the shape of a skull. "Did Darcy say what this dude's name was?"

"Charles," Carrie answered. "But she says everyone calls him Cheech."

"Cheech?" Emma repeated dubiously.

Carrie shrugged. "That's what she said."

She reached up and snapped the skull knocker.

"Molly's parents are very, very warped people," Sam said, shaking her head.

The jet-black front door swung open. A lone spotlight on the floor lit up a very tall, cadaverous-looking man wearing a black tuxedo.

"Yeeees?" he growled.

It was Simon, the butler. The girls had met him many times. He preferred to be called Lurch, like the butler in the old *Addams Family* television shows.

"Hi, Lurch," Emma said, reaching out to shake hands with him. "You know Sam and Carrie."

"Indeed I do!" Simon growled in his low, hoarse voice as he shook Emma's hand. "How's life been?"

"Good," Carrie said as Simon led them inside.

"I do hope good means hot, hot, hot," Simon intoned, "because death is going to be cold, cold, cold."

*And people think I'm strange,* Sam thought, staring at Simon.

"Is Darcy in the dining room?" Emma asked.

"Everyone will be in the dining room," Simon said. "Can you find your way there? Follow the bloody line on the floor. I have duties in the kitchen. Duties!" He threw his head back and laughed maniacally.

The three girls looked at him a little nervously.

"Uh, we can find our way," Emma assured him.

"I've got to find a bathroom," Sam said. "I'll meet you there."

"If you survive," Simon noted. Then he turned away to go to the kitchen.

Sam made her way to the bathroom that was located off the family room. It was decorated in the main Mason mansion color—black. The hand towels were covered in a pattern of bloody handprints. A coffin-shaped box held black tissues. There was a painting of a witch over the sink. A black rubber bat hung from the ceiling directly over the toilet.

"And I thought my mother had bad taste," Sam said to herself as she washed her hands.

53

Sam made her way to the dining room table, where Carrie, Emma, Molly, and Darcy were all seated. Darcy was wearing black velvet jeans and a sheer black blouse over a black lace camisole. It looked amazing on her tall, muscular frame. Her long, thick black hair was braided and held back by a black velvet ribbon.

*And look what she's done with Molly!* Sam thought. Sixteen-year-old Molly, who was confined to a wheelchair as a result of an auto accident a year and a half ago, looked fantastic. She had on a long, gauzy, red-and-gold print skirt with a matching vest.

*She looks great! In fact, this whole room looks great! Candlelight and everything!*

"Glad you could join us, Sam," Darcy said in her usual matter-of-fact tone. "Have a seat!"

Sam went to one of the two unoccupied seats at the table—the one between Emma and Carrie.

"This is too cool!" Sam exclaimed, her eyes taking in the candelabra, the fancy dishes, and the perfect crystal glassware on the table. "You don't eat like this every night, do you? Because if you do, I want to be adopted."

"No way," Molly said with a grin. "It's usually me and Darcy and a pizza with everything on it."

"Are your parents around?" Sam asked.

"Out for the evening," Molly said. "At the movies—some new horror thing."

"Checking out the competition," Darcy said with a grin.

"Hey, Car, there's your movie!" Sam cried, pointing at a poster on the wall.

Since the last time she and her friends had been to the Masons', they had redone the dining room. It now featured giant floor-to-ceiling posters from the movies they had written together. Prominently featured was an advance poster for *Sunset Beach Slaughter,* a movie that had been filmed right on the island, and in which Carrie had had a small speaking part.

"I tried to convince the movie company to use your photo," Darcy said with a grin. "But it was no deal."

"Thank God," Carrie said. "I was definitely not cut out to be an actress."

"Whereas I was," Sam said. "Maybe that

should be my new job." She looked over at Molly. "Do you think your parents could hire me on a more or less permanent basis?"

"I have no casting clout," Molly said with a smile. "Sorry."

"Story of my life," Sam said with a sigh. "So, where's Charles?"

"Cheech," Molly corrected her. "He likes to be called Cheech."

"Oh, upstairs, getting dressed," Darcy said lightly. "He'll be down in a sec. In fact, here he is now!"

A guy walked into the room. Darcy stood up, went to him, threw her arms around his neck, and gave him a passionate kiss in front of everyone.

That was bizarre enough in and of itself. Darcy was not the kind of girl to make a big public show of affection. But the way Cheech looked was even more absurd.

*This is Cheech?* Sam thought, totally shocked. *I thought this dinner was formal!*

The twentyish guy who had walked into the room was reasonably handsome, if a little on the chubby side. He was about as tall as Darcy, with curly dark hair and dark eyes.

He had a lightning-bolt earring dangling from his left ear. And a ring through his nose.

And that wasn't all. For what was supposed to be a formal dinner, he was wearing black motorcycle boots, torn jeans, and a leather jacket open practically to his navel—with no shirt underneath. His soft belly protruded a couple of inches. A tattoo on his right pec read *Born to Raise Hell*.

Darcy held his hand, her eyes dancing with happiness. "Cheech," she said, "I want you to meet my friends Sam, Emma, and Carrie."

"Hi," Sam said noncommittally.

"Nice to meet you," Carrie added, evidently trying to be friendly.

"Hello," Emma said, her voice perfectly polite.

"Yo," Cheech replied. Then he went to the lone empty seat at the table and sat down. Darcy grinned at her friends as if to say, "Isn't he the coolest?"

*I must be dreaming,* Sam thought, sneaking another peek at Cheech. *Oh, my God, is his left nipple pierced?*

Simon came into the dining room, holding a tray. "Drinks?" he asked. "We feature Campari and Bloody Marys."

"No, thanks," Emma said. "Just a club soda."

"Same for me," Carrie ordered.

"I'll have a very light screwdriver," Sam said.

Lurch reached into his apron pocket, pulled out a small screwdriver, and tossed it to Sam. Everyone cracked up, including Cheech.

"And for the gentleman?" Lurch asked.

"Gimme a Seven and Seven," Cheech said as he tried to get something out from between his teeth with the nail of his pinky. "And back me up."

"Back you up?" Lurch asked him.

"You know, fossilface," Cheech said to him sharply, "back me up! Bring me two! And keep 'em coming!"

Sam looked at Emma and Carrie. Their jaws were bouncing off the table in shock. But Darcy was looking at Cheech as if he were Keanu Reeves, Brad Pitt, and Albert

Einstein all rolled into one. And Molly was looking at him exactly the same way.

*Okay, there's only one possibility here,* Sam thought. *Darcy has lost her mind. She's been taken over by pod people or something. Molly, too.*

Simon quickly made the drinks at the dining room sideboard. He served them with a flourish, putting two 7 and 7s down in front of Cheech.

Cheech tasted one.

"You call this a drink?" he said to Simon.

"Of course," the butler answered with a dignified growl.

"This isn't a drink. This is friggin' water!"

"Cheech, baby, calm down," Darcy said to him soothingly.

"Water!" Cheech repeated. "You know what you do with water?" Without waiting for a response, he took his drink and dumped it into a floral arrangement in the middle of the table. "Water the flowers!" he yelled. "That's what you do with water!"

"Cheech," Darcy implored gently.

"Now, bring me a real drink!" he said to Simon loudly. "And back me up!"

Lurch scurried back to the sideboard. Sam snuck another glance at her friends. Their expressions were more shocked than hers. Emma was even looking kind of pale.

*Well, maybe we're not giving this guy a chance,* Sam thought, though she found it hard to convince herself. *People judge me sometimes because of how I dress. I'm not going to judge the dude. Darcy seems to like him. Maybe we just need to give him a chance.*

"So, Cheech," Sam asked, trying to be friendly, "where did you and Darcy meet?"

Cheech looked at Sam. Actually, he leered at Sam. And then he licked his lips.

"The pen," he answered.

"The what?" Sam queried, not understanding.

"The pen, the slammer, the rock yard. Prison, get it?" Cheech replied.

"You met in *prison?*"

"Actually, he's telling the truth," Darcy hastened to explain. "I'm taking a summer penology course at the university. We visited the state penitentiary. That's where Cheech and I met."

"I got out a couple of weeks ago," Cheech said proudly.

"Good," Carrie said, trying to keep up with the conversation. "What were you in for?"

"Auto theft," Cheech replied. "I borrowed my friend's car. He said I stole it. But I only borrowed it from him. It was a totally bogus thing, man."

"Anyway, the past's the past," Darcy said philosophically.

"Yeah, a few black marks," Cheech commented. "I got a few black marks. No biggie."

"I think you're wonderful, Cheech," Molly said, gazing at him fondly.

"Yeah, I know you do, babe," Cheech said, draining his first drink and reaching for the second.

*Now I know why Darcy wanted us to dress formally,* Sam thought sarcastically. *She was hoping we'd wear some expensive jewelry that Cheech could "borrow"!*

"Tell my friends what you want to do now," Darcy encouraged Cheech.

"Fix cars," Cheech said. "I learned how in prison. Fix 'em to go faster."

"So . . . do you plan on continuing your education in . . . uh, auto mechanics' school?" Emma inquired coolly.

"Education, schmeducation," Cheech said, finishing his second drink. "I figure I learn what I need from the street!"

"Lovely," Emma said with a stiff smile.

"Yo, skullface!" Cheech yelled to Simon, who had gone back to the kitchen. "I said back me up! My throat's dry!"

"So . . . uh . . . you and Darcy must have other things in common," Carrie said, once Simon had served Cheech two more drinks.

"Yeah," Cheech said, belching loudly. "We both gotta pee sometimes! Speakin' of which, whew, I gotta whiz like a racehorse!" He got up from his chair and staggered a little drunkenly toward the bathroom.

When he was gone, Sam turned to Darcy.

"I hate to say it," she said, "but you have lost your mind."

"Your boyfriend is a cretin," Emma exclaimed, for once dropping her polite demeanor.

"What do you think of him, Carrie?" Darcy asked. "I really want to know."

"He's a disgusting pig," Carrie said conversationally. "But other than that, I'm sure he's a lovely person."

"So you think he's a jerk," Darcy summed up.

"Basically," Carrie said matter-of-factly.

"Me, too," Darcy added nonchalantly.

"What?" Sam asked.

"Yeah, this Cheech character is a jerk," Darcy said smoothly. "But the videotape we've made is going to be hilarious to watch!"

*Videotape? What videotape?* Sam thought.

"Ron! Lurch!" Molly called. "Show the girls the camera!"

The butler and Cheech came back in. But this time Cheech's nose ring, earring, and nipple ring were gone, and he was dressed in a jacket and tie.

"Hi, everyone," he said in a normal voice. "My name's Ron Wilson. I'm an old friend of Darcy's from when she lived in Bangor!"

He and Simon pulled black fabric away from the far wall, revealing a still-rolling videotape camera.

"Oh, my God!" Sam yelled. "This is hilarious!"

"You were making a videotape?" Emma asked incredulously.

"Tell me this wasn't the funniest thing you've ever seen!" Molly yelled with glee. "You should have seen your faces!"

"You actually believed he was my fiancé!" Darcy said, bent over with laughter.

"Busted," Sam admitted, a big grin on her face. "I mean, we thought you were crazy, but we bought it."

"Totally," Carrie agreed.

"I can't believe you did this," Emma said.

"I can," Molly said. "We saw it on *Oprah* last week. We've been dying to try it."

"When Ron came down to visit me, bang!" Darcy said. "We planned the whole thing. Dinner's gonna be great."

"But the after-dinner entertainment's gonna be even better," Molly cracked.

Everyone at the table burst into laugher. And Sam laughed the hardest of all.

# FIVE

Sam looked up from the Tuesday morning *Press-Herald* with a satisfied look on her face.

*This is the one,* she thought. *I can just feel it. There was nothing in here yesterday, but today I've hit the employment jackpot!*

It was the morning after Darcy's dinner and Sam was still trying to find a job. The twins had already left for camp, and Dan was off at the golf course again.

And Sam had just spotted a classified ad in the newspaper that looked exceptionally promising. She put the black marker she'd been holding down on the kitchen table and reached for the phone. Marked off was the following advertisement:

### MODELS NEEDED

Fit models needed by clothes designer. One male, one female needed. Prefer tall. Legitimate. Regular hours. In Portland. Phone (207) 555-5454.

*That's the one,* Sam thought, *and the early bird gets the worm. For once, I'm going to be the early bird.*

She dialed the number listed.

"Mankin Models," a male voice answered. "Peter Mankin, may I help you?"

"I'm calling about the advertisement for fit models," Sam answered. "I hope I'm not too late."

The man laughed. "No, you're not," he said. "Hold on one moment and I'll get the boss."

Sam heard herself being put on hold. A few seconds later, another man picked up.

"Mitch Mankin," he said. "May I help you?"

*Gee, he sounds an awful lot like the guy*

*who just transferred me to him,* Sam thought. *Brothers can sound so much alike!*

"Mr. Mankin, this is Samantha Bridges," Sam said, trying to sound as businesslike as possible. "I'd like to apply for the modeling job you advertised."

"Great!" the man said. "I'm so glad my brother put you through to me."

"The job's not filled?" Sam asked, crossing her fingers for luck.

"That depends," Mitch said. "There's always room for the right model."

"Oh, that's me!" Sam said quickly. "I mean, I think that's me. I mean, I hope that's me, is what I mean."

*Shut up, Sam!* she told herself. *You sound like a total imbecile!*

"So, Samantha, tell me about yourself," Mitch said easily.

"Well, start by calling me Sam—everybody does."

"Okay, Sam," Mitch obliged. "Tell me more."

"I grew up in Junction, Kansas, but now I live on Sunset Island, and—"

"No, no, no," Mitch said quickly. "That's

67

very nice, but I mean modeling information. You got any professional experience?"

Sam debated for a moment. The previous summer, she'd had some pictures of her taken by Flash Hathaway, the famous fashion photographer. Of course, Flash had basically tricked her into posing for lingerie shots, and then had displayed them without Sam's permission.

*Should I tell him about Flash Hathaway or not?* Sam wondered. *That was technically modeling experience, but he was such a sleazeball! And I wouldn't show those photos to anyone!*

Sam decided to go for it. Maybe Mitch would recognize Flash's name.

"I did have Flash Hathaway take some photos of me. . . ."

"Flash!" Mitch said. "I know Flash. Everyone knows Flash."

"He's a good photographer," Sam said. *A total sleazeball,* she added in her mind, *but a good photographer.*

"One of the best in the business," Mitch agreed. "So far, so good. What else?"

"Well, let's see . . . Oh! I've done some runway work," Sam added suddenly, remembering that she had been in a local fashion show on the island, where she modeled a bridal gown.

"Oh, great," Mitch said. "So you really are experienced."

"Yes," Sam said quickly, nervously wrapping the phone cord around her fingers, "and I'm totally professional. I mean, I would be, if you hired me."

"So, what do you look like?"

"I'm tall," Sam said.

"Tall is good," Mitch said. "How tall?"

"About five foot ten, a hundred and eighteen pounds," Sam said, "and I have long, curly red hair. I'm a perfect size eight."

"Nice," Mitch said. "A waif look."

"Well, I don't know about that," Sam said. "I mean, I'm naturally thin, but I don't look, like, anorexic or anything."

"Uh-huh, uh-huh," Mitch said. "Is your hair naturally red? Because bad dye jobs are tacky."

"Oh, I'm a natural redhead," Sam assured him eagerly.

"Terrific," Mitch replied.

*Hey, this is really going well,* Sam thought

69

hopefully. *Oh, please let me get this job, please, please, please* . . .

"Do you have freckles?" Mitch asked.

"A few," Sam answered honestly. "But not very many, really. I'm one of those rare redheads who tan."

"Oh, so you've got a tan," Mitch said.

"Yeah," Sam replied. "Is that okay?"

"Sure, sure," Mitch said. "But the sun is bad for a model's skin. You know that, don't you?"

"I don't have any lines or anything," Sam said quickly. "I'm only nineteen."

"And your measurements?" Mitch asked briskly. "Sorry to ask, but I can't hire you without knowing your measurements."

"I'm not busty," Sam said, "if that's what you're asking."

"Could you be a little more specific?" Mitch asked.

"Well, I'm kind of . . . uh . . . small," Sam admitted.

"Small enough that you can get away without wearing a bra?" Mitch asked.

"Yeah," Sam admitted. "But that's good for a model, isn't it?"

"Sure, it's fine," Mitch said. "You don't have to be busty for this job."

"Oh, good," Sam replied with relief.

"And what kind of underwear do you like to wear?" Mitch continued, his tone not changing.

"What?" Sam asked.

"Underwear," Mitch went on. "What kind do you like to wear?"

"I don't understand," Sam said, suddenly wary.

"Bikini?" Mitch asked, and now his voice started to sound kind of funny—weird and breathy. "Schoolgirl cottons? French-cut? Or maybe none at all?"

"Go to hell!" Sam screamed into the phone, and then slammed it down. *The sick sonofabitch! That guy is a total weirdo! He probably doesn't even have a brother. He probably answers the phone himself, and then pretends to have someone else in his office! I should call the police on him! In fact, I will!*

She quickly got the number of the Portland police from information and dialed it. Then she told an officer what had happened and filed a complaint against sleazy

Mitch Mankin—or whatever his real name was.

Sam sighed and put her head down on the kitchen table. *First Flash Hathaway, then Mitch Mankin,* she thought. *I don't think I'm having a lot of luck in the modeling business!*

"Hey, big guy," Sam said later that day as she eased up behind her boyfriend and whispered in his ear. "You got a bike I can ride?"

Pres turned around and grinned. "Hey, girl!" he drawled. "I am so glad to see you. What are you doing here?" He quickly rubbed his grimy hands on a towel he kept stuffed in his back pocket.

"Seeing you," Sam cooed.

"But aren't you—"

"It's a long story," Sam replied. "When do you get off for lunch?"

"Now," Pres said.

"Let me buy you lunch," she said softly. "I'll make it worth your while."

"Let *me* buy *you* lunch," Pres replied. "I make a lot more money than you do."

Sam had spent the rest of the morning

trying, without success, to find both a job and a place to live. Finally she'd decided to bicycle over to Pres's job—he worked at Wheels, a local motorcycle shop—to see if he would have lunch with her.

"Deal, cowboy," Sam said.

"I've got a nicer place in mind than a restaurant," Pres commented.

Thirty minutes later, after buying a couple of sandwiches and some fruit and taking a short ride on Pres's motorcycle, the two of them were perched on a rocky cliff overlooking the Atlantic Ocean, hungrily devouring their sandwiches. Sam had told Pres the whole story of how she no longer was an au pair for Becky and Allie Jacobs.

"So it was over, just like that," Pres drawled, snapping his fingers on the word *that*.

"Yep," Sam said.

"Well," Pres said softly, "maybe it's for the best."

"I hope so," Sam declared.

"You're gonna miss those twins," Pres said.

"Right," Sam agreed sarcastically. "Like I'll miss Dan himself. What a jerk."

"I think he's more insecure than he is a jerk," Pres mused, biting into his sandwich.

"Like I could care less," Sam said, starting on her apple.

"You don't feel bad for those girls?" Pres asked. "No mom and Dan Jacobs for a father?"

"Yes, I do," Sam declared. "But there's not much I can do for them if I've been fired, is there?" She took another bite out of the apple.

"One thing's for sure," Pres murmured.

"What's that?" Sam asked.

"You'll have a lot more nights free now to be with me," Pres said, grinning at her.

"You won't want me," Sam said, resting the half-eaten apple on a brown paper bag. "I'll have wasted away from hunger due to lack of funds. What am I—"

But Pres cut the sentence off by kissing Sam gently on the lips.

Sam returned the kiss, and it seemed like an eternity before it was over.

"Missed me?" Pres asked.

"Oh, maybe a little," Sam told him.

"Let me help convince you," Pres said,

and he kissed her again, just as deliciously as before.

"Yep," Sam whispered when the kiss was over. "That just about does it."

Sam leaned her head against Pres's shoulder and the two of them were silent for a time, looking out at the ocean together.

"I gotta find a job," Sam finally said, "and I gotta find a place to live."

"Well," Pres said, looking down at the ocean below them, "I might be able to help you on that latter score."

Sam's heart leaped. She hadn't dared mention to Pres her idea about moving into the Flirts's house—she was impetuous, yes, but she also knew that it wasn't just up to Pres, it was up to Billy.

*But maybe Pres is going to bring it up himself. He certainly is being extremely loving this afternoon. Yes,* she prayed, *yes!*

"You know that bulletin board in the shop?" Pres asked, shifting position on the rocks and tilting his face to the sun.

"Yeah," Sam replied.

Pres was talking about a big bulletin board that was in the window of Wheels. On it were posted all kinds of notices about

what was going on around the island—
who needed a ride to Boston, who needed
their lawn cut, baby-sitter availability, that
sort of thing.

"This girl was in this morning to post a
notice," Pres drawled. "I read it."

"What about it?"

"She's sublettin' her apartment," Pres
continued. "One bedroom, a cottage kind of
thing. Cheap."

"How much?" Sam asked. "I don't have a
job yet, remember?"

"I don't remember," Pres answered. "But
I know it said it was available immediately."

"How do you know so much about this
notice?" Sam asked, wondering for a split
second what the relationship was between
Pres and this girl.

"I posted it myself," Pres said, tugging
on a lock of Sam's hair.

"Oh," Sam replied, chagrined.

"Do I detect a tad of jealousy?" Pres
asked, a grin starting to spread over his
face. "Just because the girl was incredibly
gorgeous, with a perfect body and long

blond hair. Oh, did I mention she was wearing one of those string bikinis?"

"Ha ha," Sam said. "Very funny."

"You know you have nothing to be jealous about," Pres told her.

"Of course I know that," Sam said quickly. "After all, you have me. Why even consider second best?"

"Yep, that's the false bravado of the girl I love," Pres teased.

"Hey!" Sam protested. "It isn't—"

But she didn't get to finish her sentence, because Pres was kissing her again.

And this time she was absolutely certain that he wasn't thinking about anyone but her.

# SIX

"This is the place, I guess," Carrie said, slowing the car.

"Forty-five Eastport Lane." Sam read the number on top of the roadside mailbox. "This is it!"

"Nice," Carrie commented as she drove slowly up the long driveway.

"Incredible," Sam said softly as she swung her head from side to side, taking in the surroundings.

"Too nice for you," Carrie joked.

"I doubt it," Sam retorted.

"We'll see," Carrie said. "How can you possibly afford it?"

"She said it was a sublet," Sam replied.

"And cheap! Because it's the middle of the summer."

"We'll see," Carrie repeated. "How much is it a month?"

"Four hundred," Sam answered.

"Four hundred dollars for this place?" Carrie asked, totally amazed. "How much is it usually?"

"A thousand," Sam said. "That's what the person said she's renting it for."

"Wow," Carrie breathed. She followed the driveway to the front of the main house and stopped.

"She said it's in the back," Sam reminded Carrie. Carrie put the car back in gear and continued on.

It was later that same afternoon, and Sam had talked Carrie into driving with her to go see the place that had been advertised on the bulletin board at Wheels.

"You might have lucked out," Carrie said, a touch of envy in her voice. "This place is awesome."

Carrie was right. Forty-five Eastport Lane was located in the richest area of Sunset Island, not far from the waterfront home of May Spencer-Rumsey, a New York book publisher for whom Carrie had done some work the summer before. And still, it was only ten minutes by bicycle from downtown—a fact Sam had been sure to check, since she would no longer have a car to borrow.

The front lawn was about five acres alone, and it was obvious, from where the winding driveway was heading, that the house backed right up onto the cliffs overlooking the ocean.

"There it is!" Sam cried, pointing to her left.

"It's gorgeous," Carrie said, seeing the small guest cottage to which Sam was pointing.

"In about an hour it's going to be mine!" Sam cried. "Getting fired was the best thing that ever happened to me!"

Carrie pulled the car into a parking place right outside the guest house, next to a blue BMW with California tags already parked there. Almost instantly the front door of the guest house popped open, and a woman who appeared to be in her early thirties came out and waved. She had dark hair pulled back in a severe bun and was dressed in a blue business suit, as if she were about to go address the Chamber of Commerce.

"That's her," Sam told Carrie. "Her name is Rachel Smith, she said."

"Why's she leaving this place?" Carrie asked Sam. "Because if it were mine . . ."

"Who knows?" Sam replied, reaching for the door handle. "She says she just got called to Europe to do some big computer programming thing. An emergency."

Carrie shrugged. "It sounds pretty legit," she commented.

"It is legit," Sam said quickly. "Anyway, you can see she's no flake. She's one of those dress-for-success types."

"The kind you hope you'll never be," Carrie joked.

"No kidding," Sam answered.

Rachel strode over to the car. "Good to meet you," she said to Sam with a grin as Sam got out. "I'm Rachel. Your hair's just as red as you said!"

"Nice to meet you, Rachel," Sam said, shaking the hand that Rachel offered. "This is my friend, Carrie Alden."

"I've seen your photos in the *Breakers,* right?" Rachel asked Carrie.

"Right!" Carrie said. Sam could see she was pleased and surprised that someone would have noticed her photo credits.

"You're really talented," Rachel said sincerely. "You're wonderful!"

"Thanks," Carrie replied. "I appreciate that."

"No problem," Rachel remarked. "Now, if you'll follow me, I'll show you inside and around."

Sam and Carrie followed Rachel like two ducklings behind the mother duck as Rachel gave them a quick tour of the guest house. It was small, but incredibly cozy and well appointed.

*I love this bedroom!* Sam thought as Rachel took them into it. *A huge double bed, and what a fabulous view of the ocean! Picture me and Pres on the bed, the ocean in the background. I'm here!*

The rest of the house was just as nice. There was a huge, open combined living room/dining room/kitchen, with ultramodern Swedish-style furniture and very few knicknacks.

The bathroom had a shower and a separate tub, as well as a vanity.

"Watch this," Rachel said. She flipped a switch on the tub. Instantly water came flying out of four whirlpool jets.

"Awesome," Sam said.

"And it's big enough for two," Rachel said, giving Sam a sly wink.

"I'll give you the full report," Sam said.

"Sure, if you want to write to me in Europe. Anyway, what else? Lots of closet space," Rachel pointed out. "And you can bicycle to town!"

"This is just incredible," Carrie said. She looked like she was falling as much in love with the place as Sam was.

"So," Rachel said when they'd made their way back into the living room, "anything else I can show you?"

Sam shook her head. She had been totally and thoroughly dazzled.

*Please, please, please, make this place mine. Please, please, please,* she thought. *I'll find some way to pay for it. I know I will.*

"So," Rachel said, taking Sam lightly by

the arm and steering her gently to the table, "let's talk some business."

Sam, Carrie, and Rachel all sat down at the big table. Rachel popped open a brief-case and pulled out some papers. "Want it?" she asked.

Sam laughed. "Is the Pope Catholic?"

"It's perfect for you," Rachel said warmly. "I'm glad it's going to be yours. You under-stand the terms of the sublet, how it's going to work?"

Sam understood. Rachel had explained it all to her on the phone when Sam first called her.

*I'm supposed to pay my rent right to the owners,* Sam recalled. *And when the phone, water, and electric bills come, I handle them like they're my own. They're totally paid up—she even said I could call the phone company to check. I just have to pay her two hundred dollars now to cover the time until the rent is due again. And then the rent is only four hundred a month! And the furniture stays with the place. And I can move in tonight!*

*I don't even care that it's going to take*

*practically all the money I have saved. I
just have to live here!*

"When can I meet the owners?" Sam
asked.

"They're out of town," Rachel said quickly.
"But they've okayed the whole thing. Look!"

She thrust a piece of paper in front of
Sam. It was a notarized letter to Rachel
Smith from Mrs. Irene Lawrence, at the
same address as the main house, okaying
the sublet.

Sam looked at Carrie. "Seem okay?"

"Yes," Carrie said, "everything seems
great!"

"Then let's do it," Sam declared. She
reached into her backpack and took out
two hundred dollars.

"Cash okay?" Sam asked Rachel, a smile
on her face.

"Perfect," Rachel said. "Now, just sign
these sublet papers."

Sam scanned the contract that Rachel
had given her. There didn't seem to be any
problems—the contract was written in En-
glish plain enough for Sam to understand.

Carrie touched Sam's arm. "Maybe you

should have Jane or Jeff Hewitt look at those papers before you sign them."

"You think?" Sam asked, biting her lower lip.

"I have to tell you I've already had another offer," Rachel said. "After you called me. As much as I'd like to sublet the place to you, I really can't hold it for you, if you're not sure. . . ."

Sam took out a pen and quickly signed both copies of the sublet agreement. "I'm sure it's fine," she said as she wrote. "I refuse to let someone else get this place!"

"One for me," Rachel said, taking one of the agreements and pushing the other one toward Sam, "and one for you." She reached her hand out to Sam again to shake to seal the deal, and Sam took it warmly.

"You are so lucky, Sam," Carrie said.

"I'm telling you, the best thing that happened to me was Dan Jacobs firing me!" Sam said with a laugh.

"You can move in after nine tonight," Rachel said. "I'll be gone by then."

"You sure?" Sam asked.

"Absolutely," Rachel replied. "I've got a ten o'clock flight to catch at Portland airport, and a midnight flight from Boston to Paris. Look, I've got one more thing to show you. Follow me."

Rachel led the way over to the refrigerator and opened it.

The fridge was sparkling clean and empty—except for a bottle of good champagne and two glasses chilling on the top shelf.

"I had such a good feeling about you on the phone," Rachel said, "I went and got these. Enjoy!"

"Wow, this is incredible!" Sam squealed. "I am totally psyched!"

"I hope you enjoy the place as much as I have," Rachel said with a kind smile.

"Okay, so I'll be back after nine," Sam promised, "if my friend Carrie is kind enough to . . ."

"You got it," Carrie said. "I'll help you."

"Great!" Rachel said happily. "Good luck here!"

As Sam and Carrie were leaving Sam couldn't help thinking that the world worked in strange ways. Two days before, she'd been fired from her job. Now it looked like she had found the greatest place to live in the entire state of Maine.

And all she had to do was find a way to afford it.

"Mom?" Sam said into the phone. "It's me, Sam!"

"Sam!" her mother exclaimed into the phone. "What a surprise!"

Sam leaned back on the couch of her new place. It was eleven o'clock at night—just ten o'clock back in Junction, Kansas, where her parents and younger sister lived. And Sam was so happy with her new surroundings that she was calling everyone she knew.

"How are you, Mom?" Sam asked. "I haven't spoken to you guys in a while."

"Great, Sam," her mother answered. "Kansas is the same, as you can imagine."

"I've moved," Sam said quickly. "I have a new number."

"You're not taking care of those girls anymore?" her mother asked, concern in her voice.

"Nope," Sam said happily. "I've got my own place. It's great!"

"But what happened to your job?" Mrs.

Bridges asked her daughter after Sam had given her the new address and phone number.

"I . . . uh . . ." Sam had to think quickly. *I don't want to tell her I got fired, even if it wasn't my fault. She'll freak.* "I'm . . . working at the Play Café as a waitress!"

"So you changed jobs, then."

Sam took a sip from the can of Coke she was holding. "I needed to make more money, Mom," she said. "You can't make any real money as an au pair."

"I suppose not," Mrs. Bridges said, hesitating. "But aren't you leaving that nice man you were working for high and dry?"

*Ha. Some nice man,* Sam thought. "He's fine with it," Sam told her mom. "And I'm doing great. How's Dad?"

"Good," Mrs. Bridges said. "He's at a preseason football meeting."

"Figures," Sam said. Mr. Bridges was the local high-school football coach.

"Did Ruth Ann call you?"

"No, I don't think so," Sam replied. *My sister, calling me? My sister hasn't called me since I left home.*

"She has some really exciting news!" Mrs. Bridges said happily.

"She's getting married," Sam guessed.

"Lordy, no," Mrs. Bridges replied. "Both you girls are too young to get married. I want to see you get an education first."

"If that was a dig about my dropping out of college, I don't appreciate it," Sam said.

"Maybe you'll decide to go back to school," Sam's mom said.

"Maybe," Sam said, eager to end that line of conversation. "So, anyway, what about Ruth Ann? She going out with some incredibly fine guy or something?"

"Ruth Ann doesn't want a boyfriend," Mrs. Bridges said.

"She's in eleventh grade, Mom," Sam reminded her mother. She tapped a fingernail on her Coke can. "It's okay if Ruth Ann wants a boyfriend."

"Well, she doesn't," her mother said. "But she did get the highest grade on her summer-school calculus final."

"Great, Mom," Sam said weakly. Ruth Ann was a major brain.

"That means she can take advanced-placement calculus next year!" her mother said happily. "There are already colleges trying to recruit her."

"To play football?" Sam asked facetiously.

"Academic," her mother said. "Academic." Then Mrs. Bridges sighed.

*It's starting again,* Sam thought. *My mother is bummed out that I quit college. And she's dying for me to go back, to become a perfect little student like perfect little Ruth Ann. Well, I've got nothing against calculus . . . but not for me! And I wouldn't want Ruth Ann's life for all the A grades in the world!*

"You know, Kansas State would probably still take you back, dear—"

"Mom," Sam said, "I'm not going back to Kansas State. And that's final."

"Some other nice college, then," Mrs. Bridges said. "I could send away for some catalogues—"

"Good, Mom," Sam said, now wanting more than anything else in the world to end this conversation. She clicked the receiver twice. "Oops!" she said quickly. "Call waiting. Gotta see who it is. Bye, Mom!"

"Bye, dear," Mrs. Bridges said. "We love you."

Sam hung up the phone and sat back on the couch.

*I love you, too, Mom,* she thought. *But I wish you'd accept me for who I am, and not keep trying to make me into who you want me to be.*

# SEVEN

*Gotta get a job*, Sam chanted to herself. *Gotta get a job. Gotta get a good job.*

Sam walked along the sunny boardwalk near the main beach by herself—Emma and Carrie were both at the country club, doing their usual au pair duties—and considered her situation carefully.

*On the one hand, my living situation is great,* she thought. *That place I moved into last night is the coolest. But if I don't get a job, I'll never be able to afford to stay there!*

So Sam had gotten up at about ten-thirty in the morning, dressed in black shorts and a sleeveless black denim shirt over her red bikini—in case she got a

95

chance to do some sunbathing—and bicycled over to the boardwalk. It was her idea to walk along the boardwalk and try to get hired at one of the many restaurants, open-air eateries, and game booths there.

But so far it had been a big zero.

"Not hiring."

"Don't need anyone."

"You can leave an application, but don't call us, we'll call you."

"Full up."

"Forget it."

"Uh-uh."

Sam had heard every turn-down in the book. Now it was twelve o'clock, and she was starting to get a little bit desperate.

She continued walking along. Five minutes later it looked like luck was finally with her.

HELP WANTED! read the hand-lettered sign at one of the amusement booths. Sam went over to check it out.

It was the Soak the Sap booth, where people tried to throw a football through a moving automobile tire about twenty feet away. If the contestant was successful, a person who was on a platform above a big pool of ocean water got dunked into it with a big splash.

The booth, which was hardly doing any business at all, was run by a middle-aged man who looked like an old hippie. He wore a tie-dyed Grateful Dead T-shirt and baggy drawstring pants. He had long flowing gray hair and a bandanna that looked like an American flag tied around his head pirate-style.

"Hi, I'm Samantha Bridges," Sam said, walking over to the booth and leaning against its front. "Your sign interests me."

"Oh, yeah?" the proprietor asked. "I'm Iron Eagle. I'm a Leo."

"What?" Sam asked, bewildered.

"My name," the man said, "is Iron Eagle. My zodiac sign is Leo, man."

"Why would I care?" Sam asked.

"You just asked me my sign," Iron Eagle said.

"I was talking about your help-wanted sign."

"Oh, yeah, sure, far out," Iron replied. "I thought you were trying to pick me up. But that's cool. Call me Iron."

"You need help here, Iron?" Sam inquired.

"Yeah," Iron said. "Help."

*Gee, he doesn't seem to have a very advanced vocabulary,* Sam thought.

"Well," Sam said, "I'm looking for a job. I can start anytime."

"Yeah?" Iron asked again.

"Yeah."

"Well," Iron said, giving Sam a look from head to toe, "you'll do."

*Okay, I'm not going to say anything about that sleazy once-over he just gave me, because I really, really, really need a job.* She took a deep breath. "So, Iron," she said, trying to sound friendly, "what's the deal? And what's the pay?"

"The deal is, you're the sap," Iron said, folding his arms. "And the pay is minimum wage, plus commission."

"I'm the sap?" Sam repeated doubtfully. "You mean I'm the person who goes flying into the water?"

"Yeah," Iron said. "What did you say your name was, sweetie?"

"It's Sam, not sweetie," Sam replied. "So

I'm supposed to, like, let people throw footballs at me and dunk me in the water?"

"Yeah," Iron said.

*I'm desperate, but I'm not that desperate,* Sam said to herself. *Talk about your major humiliation.* "Thanks anyway, Iron, but I'm not into it." She turned to leave. No way was she going to be the sap.

"Hey, wait a sec," Iron called to Sam. Sam stopped in her tracks.

"Don't jump to conclusions," he continued. "C'mere, I'll show ya."

Sam watched as Iron Eagle climbed the ladder up to the platform above the small, deep dunking pool filled with chilly ocean water. He made his way out onto a platform and lay down.

"Flip the switch, man," he said, pointing.

Sam saw the white switch he was talking about and flipped it. Instantly a couple of automobile tires hanging on metal chains starting moving along a metal track.

"Now try to throw a football through one of the tires," Iron said.

Sam picked up a football, aimed, and fired. She missed by about two feet. She tried again, with the same result. And again and again and again.

"See what I mean?" Iron asked. "No one ever dunks ya."

"No wonder you don't do any business," Sam muttered.

She flipped the switch off as Iron climbed down.

"So, you want the gig?" Iron asked her.

"Not enough money," Sam decided.

"There's commissions," Iron reminded her.

"What commissions?" Sam asked.

"You're a good-lookin' chick," Iron said. "Lots of people are gonna want to try to dunk you. It's three throws for a buck. I'll give you a quarter for every two bucks spent."

Sam did some quick calculations in her mind.

*If twenty people throw at me an hour, and they each spend two bucks, I'll make five dollars in commission alone!* she thought. *And my regular pay. Okay. I can do this. I get to just sit there and look cute.*

"When do I start?" Sam asked.

"You got a suit on underneath?" Iron asked.

100

Sam nodded.

"Now," Iron said. "Get on up there."

Sam pulled off her outer clothing and climbed up the ladder to the platform. Iron immediately put on a Jefferson Airplane tape from the 1960s and cranked the music up loud. Then he began a carnival-barker spiel.

"Hey, step right up, soak the sap, soak the sap," he cried in the voice of a true carnie. "Cute babe, cute babe, soak her, soak her, get her all wet!"

Sam smiled and waved to the people walking by on the boardwalk. *Okay, so it isn't exactly show business,* she admitted to herself. *But someday I'll be able to write about this in my memoirs. And it'll make a great anecdote to tell for my* Lifestyles of the Rich and Famous *interview. . . .*

"Come one, come all, soak the babe in the bikini!" Iron called in his loud, obnoxious voice. "Soak the sap!"

A crowd started to gather. And people began to try their luck. Sam was nervous at first, but she soon saw that nobody could actually get the football through the moving tires, and she relaxed.

*Easiest job I ever had,* she crowed to herself as she basked in the noonday sun. *I'm gonna get paid to work on my tan. Jeez, I should have put on sunblock. . . .*

"Sam! Hey, Sam!" Sam heard a familiar voice call to her. She looked around. It was Allie Jacobs. She was leading a bunch of younger kids from the day camp on some sort of walk along the boardwalk.

"Allie!" Sam yelled back, and waved.

"This is your job?" Allie asked, astonished.

"Yep," Sam cried.

"Bet it sucks!" Allie shouted cheerfully.

"Well," Sam called, "it's a job!"

"We hate it at home!" Allie shouted. "Kiki is being a total twit!"

"Hang in there!" Sam yelled.

"We miss you!" Allie called as she continued walking. "We haaaaaate her!"

"Bye!" Sam called. She felt a tiny twinge at seeing Allie, almost as if . . . she actually missed her.

"Nah, impossible," Sam said out loud.

*Of course, it was a lot more fun hanging out by the pool at the ritzy country club with Emma and Carrie than it is hanging out up here.*

"Soak the sap!" Iron yelled. "Step right up, young and old. Try to hit the honey in the itty-bitty bikini!"

"Maybe you could leave off the endearments," Sam said, leaning over toward Iron.

Iron shrugged. "Hey, step right up, soak the sap, soak the sap."

"Uh, Iron?"

"I run the booth, okay?" Iron told Sam. "I'm trying to make a profit here, or else how can I afford to pay you?" He turned back to the crowd. "Soak the babe, really cute babe, soak her, soak her, get her all wet!"

"Oh, yoo-hoo, Sammy!"

Sam groaned. She looked down at the boardwalk. There, together, were her two archenemies on the island—Lorell Courtland, who had just called to her in her syrupy Georgia accent, and Diana De Witt.

And they were with two drop-dead gorgeous, to-die-for guys. One was tall and blond with a buzz cut and a great tan, and the other one was shorter with curly dark hair. Both were muscular and in great shape.

*The two-headed she-devil from hell,* Sam thought. *Those girls exist to make my life miserable. And Emma's life and Carrie's life, too. And since they're such jerks, why do they have to look so great in their bathing suits?*

Diana had on a crocheted white bikini and Lorell had on a violet maillot with high-cut legs.

"New job, Sam?" Diana called with malicious sweetness.

"I guess the last one baby-sittin' was too difficult for her little brain to handle!" Lorell trilled.

"Well, this one might be too difficult for her little chest to handle!" Diana quipped, and the entire group she was with convulsed with laughter.

"We heard you were demoted," Lorell cooed.

"Fired," Diana said.

"Bye-bye, baby-sittin'," Lorell added.

"So you found a job more suited to your skills!" Diana yelled, cracking up.

"Why don't you try to soak me, then?" Sam cried, getting angry.

*Nothing would make me happier than to take these guys for fifteen or twenty bucks,* she thought. *Make them pay the hard way.*

"What a good idea!" Diana said. Sam watched as she conferred with Lorell and the two guys for a minute. Then the blond-haired guy with the buzz cut stepped up to Iron Eagle, took a ten-dollar bill out of his wallet, and took one of the footballs.

"How many throws for ten bucks?" he asked.

"Thirty," Iron Eagle said, grinning. "Thirty throws. You're my kind of customer, man."

Iron Eagle flicked the white switch, and the tires started moving on the track. Sam watched as the guy pulled the football up to his shoulder and let fly. A direct hit . . .

*Splash!*

Sam sputtered as she hit the water hard. When she stood up, her hair dripped in her face. She pushed it back, trying to maintain some dignity, while Diana, Lorell, and the two guys laughed hysterically.

"Beginner's luck," Sam grumbled, and waded over to the ladder, which she mounted. In no time, she was ready again on her perch.

The guy threw again.

*Splash!* Sam slammed into the water.

"Yeah, we got a champ here," Iron Eagle chortled as Sam climbed back up to her perch. "Go again, big guy."

*Splash!*

"Hey, Sammy!" Lorell called.

"Yeah?" Sam mumbled, incensed.

"Twenty-seven more throws to go!"

Diana added, "You know who this guy is?"

Sam didn't answer.

"The quarterback of the Boston College football team!" Diana cried.

*Oh, no,* Sam thought as she climbed gamely up the ladder again. *I am in for a long afternoon. A really, really long afternoon.*

*A shower,* Sam thought as she pulled her bicycle into the driveway of 45 Eastport Lane. *My life for a shower!*

Sam had quit her job at the Soak the Sap

106

booth after the quarterback of the Boston College football team had dunked her for the seventh consecutive time. She'd just climbed out of the pool, put on her clothes, and walked away. Iron Eagle had screamed at her, and Diana and Lorell had ribbed her unmercifully, but Sam didn't care.

*I'd rather eat dirt than go back there,* Sam vowed to herself as she trudged up to her new house. *So what if I tried every other place on the boardwalk and no one hired me? There's always tomorrow.*

"I am so exhausted," Sam said out loud. "I need a Pres massage, that's what I need. Maybe I'll call him later."

*I'm also tired, salty, sweaty, and broke,* she added to herself as she unlocked her front door. *Forget the shower! I'm thinking Jacuzzi!*

But when Sam went inside, stripped down to nothing, and turned on the water for the Jacuzzi, nothing came out of the jets.

*Weird,* she thought. *I'll have to call the water company.*

She went into the living room to try to

find the phone directory. She flipped the wall switch and—

And nothing happened. No lights went on. She went to another light switch and flipped it.

Nothing. And then another, and another, and another. There was no electricity in the house.

*What is going on here?* Sam wondered. She went to the telephone and picked it up, intent on calling directory assistance.

The phone was dead.

*I have no phone, no electricity, and no water,* Sam thought. *This really sucks! I'm going over to the main house to ask Mrs. Lawrence if I can use her phone. She's supposed to be back from her trip today!*

Sam dressed again and went over to the main house, so angry that she was practically fuming. She rang the doorbell. When the door opened a woman in her late fifties peered out.

"Who are you?" she demanded.

"I'm Sam Bridges," Sam said. "I'm subletting the guest house."

"You're *what?*" the woman said.

"Subleting," Sam repeated. "The guest house. From Rachel Smith."

"There isn't any Rachel Smith living there!" the woman said. "I rented that place to Penelope Ann Callender. Now, who are you?"

"Sam Bridges! Look, I did sublet that cottage—"

"I am going to have to call the police!" the woman declared.

"Wait!" Sam said, a sick feeling rising in the pit of her stomach.

The woman peered at her closely. "What?" she asked warily.

"Did Penelope drive a car with California plates?" Sam asked her hesitantly.

"Why, yes!" the woman said. "She's living in my guest house."

The sick feeling in Sam's stomach got worse. "No, she isn't," Sam said quietly. "She sublet it to me."

"She did no such thing!" the woman replied. "She's not allowed to sublet. It says so clearly in her lease."

For a moment the world started to spin for Sam, she was so upset.

It all made sense. Rachel Smith and

Penelope Ann Callender. And the phone not working anymore, and the water and electricity being turned off.

*Penelope skipped town, with my two hundred bucks, and without paying her bills!* Sam realized. *She totally ripped me off!*

"Mrs. Lawrence?" Sam asked finally. "Can I come in? Because I think I can explain everything."

# EIGHT

"I'm gonna ask him," Sam declared. "How can he possibly refuse me?" She smiled and pushed back the chair she was sitting on so it was resting on its rear legs.

"Are you sure you're doing the right thing?" Emma asked dubiously.

"Well, considering that at the moment my entire life is totally messed up, I don't think I have much choice," Sam pointed out.

It was later that same evening—the evening Sam had learned that her sublet at 45 Eastport Lane had been a giant rip-off by Penelope Ann Callender, or Rachel Smith.

*Or whatever her name really is,* Sam thought disgustedly. *I'd like to wrap my hands around her preppy little neck and squeeze until she turns blue.*

Sam had bicycled over to the Hewitts' house to talk over her horrendous day with Emma, who was home baby-sitting for little Katie for the evening. The two of them were hanging out up in Emma's room, and Katie was fast asleep down the hall in her own room.

"When do you plan to ask Pres about this?" Emma asked. She sat back on her bed and pulled her knees up to her chest.

"Tonight," Sam decided. "I'm going over to the Flirts's house just as soon as Pres gets off work. And I'll pop the question!"

*I'd better go over there,* Sam thought. *Because if I can't convince Pres and Billy to let me move in with them, this girl from Kansas is going to end up sleeping under the boardwalk!*

"That's in about twenty-five minutes," Emma said, looking at her watch.

"I'm just going to have to be my most lovable," Sam commented.

"Well, you're usually lucky," Emma observed. "You got lucky once tonight."

Sam, who'd been sitting on the desk chair in Emma's room, got up and moved over to join Emma on the bed. "How's that?" she asked.

"That woman's letting you stay at the Eastport Lane house tonight," Emma said.

"I pleaded for mercy," Sam said wryly. "And I would not call the day I had lucky. I would call it hell, I would call it a nightmare, but I would not call it lucky."

"I wish I'd been there to see you convince her to let you stay," Emma said, shaking her head.

"It made her day," Sam joked. "I *was* charm."

"Charm didn't seem to work over at Soak the Sap," Emma teased.

Earlier Sam had told Emma the whole story of her misadventure with Iron Eagle and Diana and Lorell on the boardwalk. At the time the incident happened, it had seemed awful. But as Sam told the story, and then ended up comparing it to the nightmare of her living situation, the two of them had wound up laughing until tears came to their eyes.

"I'm nominating you for my old job tomorrow," Sam suggested. "I hear there's a vacancy at the very, very top."

"I'll pass," Emma said.

"That guy gives the boardwalk a bad name," Sam observed. "Plus he's seriously stuck in the sixties."

"I can't stand tie-dye," Emma said with a shrug.

"Yeah, it never has a designer label."

Emma made a face. "I can't afford designer labels anymore."

"That's okay, Em," Sam said. "You could make a paper bag look expensive." She reached into the bag of chips at her feet. "So," she said, swinging the subject of the conversation back to her housing situation, "do you think I have a chance?"

"With Pres?" Emma asked.

"Of course with Pres," Sam said. "Who else would I be talking about?"

"Maybe," Emma said noncommittally.

"Maybe?" Sam repeated. "That's the best hope you can offer me? Girlfriend, give me confidence!"

114

Emma reached for an earring that was sitting on her nightstand and started playing with it absent-mindedly. "Well, there's a lot to think about."

"Like what?" Sam challenged. "I present myself, he says yes, we live happily ever after."

"It's not that simple," Emma continued. "Have you thought about what the living arrangement would be like over there?"

"No," Sam answered honestly. "What's to think about? Hey, I ate all the chips," she added, shaking the empty bag. Emma threw her a bag of Doritos that was lying on the bed.

"Maybe you'd better start thinking about it," Emma suggested.

"What do you mean?" Sam asked, breaking open the Doritos bag. "Like do I get my own bathroom?"

"It's not that simple," Emma said, trying to be serious with Sam.

"Yes, it is," Sam said flippantly. "Mmmm, these Doritos are dee-lish."

"No, it isn't," Emma said. "Where are you going to sleep?"

"You mean sleep as in not conscious, or sleep as in hot sex?" Sam asked.

"I guess that depends on what *you* mean," Emma said with a meaningful glance.

"Okay," Sam said. "Well, we all know that Pres and I are not . . ."

"Right," Emma agreed. "And you shouldn't start just because of this."

"Yes, Miss I'm-Staying-a-Virgin-Until-I-Get-Married," Sam teased her. "Pres and I will hang from chandeliers when I'm ready, and not before. So I'll sleep on their couch."

"That incredibly funky couch in the Flirts's living room?" Emma asked.

"I'll put sheets down, I'll fumigate, what's the big deal?"

Emma nodded. "And you think that will be okay with Pres and Billy?"

"Yeah, I guess," Sam said, hesitating for just a minute. "I mean, why not?"

"Why not?" Emma asked. "Don't you think Pres is going to want you in his bed?"

"But we aren't—" Sam protested.

"I *know* that," Emma said, cutting her off, "but now you're asking him if you can move in with him."

"Not *with* him," Sam corrected. "Into his

house. Besides, Pres isn't the kind of guy to put strings on it and you know it."

Just then the phone rang. Emma picked it up.

"Hewitt residence," she said, "Emma Cresswell speaking."

It was Carrie, who was home baby-sitting for little Chloe Templeton.

"You want Carrie in on this big decision of yours?" Emma asked Sam, holding her hand over the receiver.

"Sure," Sam said. "The more the merrier!"

Emma told Sam to go downstairs and pick up the cordless phone so that the three girls could talk together. By the time Sam had gone downstairs, found the phone, and then come back upstairs, Emma had brought Carrie up to date on Sam's plan.

"You sure about this, Sam?" Carrie asked.

"No and yes," Sam replied.

"What does that mean?" Emma asked.

"No, I'm not sure," Sam explained, "but if I don't do it, yes, I'm totally screwed! I have one night in a cottage with no lights, no phone, and no running water. I am out two hundred bucks. It's not like I have a ton of options."

"I wish I could put you here," Carrie said. "There's a ton of room."

"Well, you can't," Sam declared.

"Carrie," Emma said, "I'm just worried about what it might do to Sam and Pres's relationship."

"Nothing," Sam said quickly. "It won't do anything."

"Don't be so sure," Carrie cautioned her. "You're going to be living together."

"No, we're not!" Sam said. "Living together is, like, two people sharing a house, and sharing their meals, and sharing the bathroom, and . . ."

Here Sam's voice trailed off.

"Exactly," Carrie said after a moment or two of quiet. "And sleeping together."

"Maybe this is the time," Sam said thoughtfully as she nibbled on yet another Dorito. "Maybe this is how it's supposed to happen."

"Not if you're not ready," Carrie cautioned Sam again.

"I agree with Carrie," Emma said, looking down at Sam at the end of her bed.

"God, do the two of you always have to be so mature and reasonable?" Sam asked. "It's really disgusting."

"Hey, we're not trying to tell you what to do," Carrie began.

"If I could just win the lottery," Sam moaned. "Tonight! How fast can you collect on that thing?"

"Sam, you didn't even buy a ticket," Emma pointed out.

"Bummer," Sam said.

"You should do what you want, Sam," Carrie said. "You know we're with you, no matter what."

"What I want is a place to sleep with hot and cold running water!" Sam exclaimed. Her two friends laughed.

She thought a moment. "Okay," Sam finally said. "I guess I want to see if I can live with Pres without living with Pres, if you know what I mean."

"Leave it to Sam," Emma said, "to do it her way."

"Well," Carrie commented, "we'll have to see what Pres and Billy say."

"I suppose," Sam said with finality, "there's just one way to find out."

*     *     *

"I need a place to sleep with hot and cold running water!" Sam told Pres as the two of them sat at the kitchen table of the Flirts's house.

Sam had bicycled over to the Flirts's house directly from Emma's. Pres was already there when she arrived, since he'd gotten off work a half-hour early. He had greeted her warmly—and had been surprised to see her, since he didn't know anything about what had happened on Eastport Lane earlier in the day. Sam brought him up to date in a hurry, but still hadn't asked him whether she might be able to move in with Billy and him.

"You got a way of makin' lightning strike you," Pres said with a grin.

"That's why you love me." Sam smiled, taking a sip of the glass of water Pres had gotten for her.

"So what exactly are you proposin'?" Pres asked. "Seein' as how you're stuck worse than a dog that just rassled with a porcupine."

"I just love those quaint Tennessee expressions," Sam said, grinning.

"You ain't gonna be able to charm little ol' me," Pres said softly, but Sam could see a smile play at the corners of his mouth.

*He knows,* Sam thought, her heart leaping with happiness. *He knows what I'm going to ask him. And he's going to say yes! I just know it!*

"Well," Sam said, moving her water glass around a little nervously, "I was wondering if I might be able to stay here—temporarily—with you guys."

"What's temporarily?" Pres asked, his grin getting wider now.

"Oh," Sam mused, "till the end of the summer."

"So," Pres said, a big smile on his face, "you want us to live together, even if we've never slept together before."

"Something like that," Sam agreed.

"Unusual," Pres commented.

"I'm an unusual girl," Sam said.

"I knew that when I first laid eyes on you," Pres drawled.

"Right back atcha, big guy." Sam grinned.

"Well," Pres said, "I don't know. . . ."

"You don't?" Sam asked, her heart beating rapidly.

"It's not up to me," Pres continued.

"Of course it is," Sam said.

"No, it isn't," Pres stated. "I have a roommate."

"Billy."

"Right," said Pres. "Even if I say yes, Billy's going to have to say okay."

"So," Sam said, smiling her most winning smile again, "do *you* say yes?"

"Yes—" Pres agreed.

"Hurray!" Sam cried. She got up from the table and threw her arms around Pres.

"Not so fast," Pres said quickly. "Yes, but on a trial basis."

"Whatever you say," Sam said, relieved.

"The trial basis is for a week," Pres continued. "You pay a third of the expenses in the house."

"Agreed."

"Which means you have to find a job," Pres said.

"Tomorrow," Sam promised. *I don't know where or how, but I'll find something.*

"And where are you planning to sleep?" Pres asked softly, his tone changing. "Because if you wanted to stay with me, that'd be good. Great, even."

Sam was quiet.

"I'd like that," Pres continued.

Sam looked deep into his eyes. "I'm not sure," she said. "I'm just not sure."

Pres took a deep breath. "Well, if you're not sure," he said, "you ain't even gettin' *close* to my bedroom. You agreed?"

"Yeah," Sam agreed, grinning at him. "Did I ever mention that you are a very, very cool guy?"

"You'll sleep on the couch in the living room," Pres said. "And you'll *stay* on the couch in the living room. Because I don't want to tempt fate."

"But—"

"Don't kid yourself or me, girl," Pres drawled. "I'm still your boyfriend. But I ain't a monk."

"To know me is to love me?" Sam asked meekly.

Pres laughed. "I guess so."

"You'll talk Billy into this?" Sam asked him.

"I'll ask Billy," was all Pres would say. "Give me the number of that woman on Eastport Lane, and I'll call you there in the morning."

He leaned over to Sam and kissed her gently.

"We both must be out of our minds," he said softly when the kiss ended.

"You, maybe," Sam quipped. "Me? I'm sane."

When Sam woke up the next morning, the first thing she saw when she went to the front door was a handwritten note from Mrs. Lawrence that had been taped to the door.

Sam—

A Presley Travis telephoned this morning to say that you're in, whatever that means. Good luck, Sam. I have the feeling you're going to need it. Lock the door and put the keys in the mailbox when you leave.

Mrs. Lawrence

# NINE

*Finally,* Sam thought as she locked her bicycle to one of the parking meters on Main Street, *some good luck. This could turn out to be great!*

It was two days later. Sam had moved into the Flirts's house and had slept, as she and Pres had worked out, on the couch. Then, the next morning, she'd woken up as early as possible and gotten on the telephone, calling everyone that she had ever met on the island to see if they knew of a job.

And finally she'd gotten lucky.

*When I called Lila Cantor at the Cheap Boutique,* Sam recalled as she strolled toward the boutique, *I didn't think I had a chance—there's practically no turnover at her store. But one of her people quit yesterday. And I've got an interview now! I just absolutely have to get this job. Everything depends on it.*

She looked down at the outfit she'd picked out, hoping it was the right thing to wear. All the salesgirls at the Cheap Boutique were incredibly hip and trendy, just like the clothes they sold.

Sam had on a hot-pink slip dress with a red and pink striped T-shirt underneath, and her lucky red cowboy boots on her feet. She'd put some of her hair into tiny braids, which she'd fastened with pink beads.

"You can get this, Sam," she told herself out loud. Then she took a deep breath and opened the door to the store. *Just remember, act as if you are totally confident, no matter what.*

"Hey, Sam!" Erin Kane called as Sam walked in.

"Yo, Kane!" Sam replied with a wave. "You know I got an interview?"

"Lila told me," Erin said happily. "I hope you get the job!"

"We'll rule!" Sam promised her friend, pumping her fist into the air.

"Absolutely!" Erin agreed with a grin.

Erin was the girl with whose father Emma and Carrie had concocted Sunset Magic perfume. She had recently been hired to replace Diana De Witt as one of the Flirts's backup singers. She was even dating Jake Fisher, the Flirts's temporary—or maybe permanent—drummer.

Erin had wild blond hair—as wild as Sam's, maybe even more so—and was really curvy and attractive, despite being a size eighteen. She always dressed in hot outfits that flattered her voluptuous build. That day, for example, she had on a black A-line minidress with lipstick-red kiss marks around the hem, and black combat boots.

"Terrific outfit," Sam said, looking her over.

"Oh, thanks," Erin said. "You, too."

"Maybe I should have worn something I bought here," Sam said anxiously. "Lila would probably like that. . . ."

"It doesn't matter," Erin said. "Hardly anything in here fits me, and she hired me.

Hey, someone was in today looking at one of your creations." She pointed to the Sam-styles dress that was hanging on a mannequin to her right.

"Did they buy it?" Sam asked her. "Please, please, tell me they bought it, because I am beyond broke."

"Nopers," Erin said. "But she said she's still interested, so maybe she'll come back in today."

"I can dream," Sam said with a sigh.

"Lila's in back," Erin said, pointing the way. "She's expecting you."

"Cool," Sam said.

"You'll do great!" Erin called to Sam.

Sam gave Erin a quick thumbs-up without turning around, then went into the stockroom area of the boutique. She headed over to Lila's door—she'd been there before, so she knew which one it was—and rapped on it twice.

"Come in!" a voice called from inside.

Sam opened the door.

"Sam Bridges," Lila Cantor said to her warmly, "good to see you. Have a seat." Sam sat.

Lila looked the same as Sam remembered her. She was about five foot five, with hair the same red color as Sam's. But where Sam's hair was wild and long, Lila's was cut very short and very chic. And, as usual, she was impeccably dressed—this time in a short beige silk dress with a matching jacket.

"So," Lila said, "you're looking for a job."

"That's right," Sam said.

"And you want to work here," Lila said.

"That's right," Sam repeated.

"You're hired," Lila replied.

"That's it?" Sam asked, astonished that she didn't even have to fill out an application or anything.

"That's it," Lila confirmed, reaching in her desk for some tax forms and pushing them across the table. "Fill these out."

"I'm really hired?" Sam asked again. "Really?"

Lila laughed. "Really. I know you, I like you, you have great style, and you know clothes."

"What's the pay?" Sam asked.

"Five-fifty an hour base salary," Lila said, quickly writing some things down on some forms of her own, "plus commission."

*Uh-oh*, Sam thought. *Iron Eagle told me about a job with commission, and I know where that got me.*

"What's the commission?" Sam asked.

"Two percent of what you sell," Lila said. "Sell a thousand dollars in merchandise, you make twenty dollars."

"That's fantastic!" Sam said. "I can do that!"

"When can you start?" Lila asked her, putting her pencil down.

"Anytime," Sam answered.

"How about now?" Lila asked with a grin. "You're dressed for the job just fine. Go on out there. Erin will train you."

"Thanks!" Sam said. "Thank you so much!"

"Oh!" Lila called, just as Sam was about to leave the office. "There's one condition."

"What's that?" Sam asked, her heart sinking a little as she turned to face her new boss.

"No conflicts of interest," Lila said firmly.

"What do you mean?" Sam questioned, not understanding.

"You're not here to sell Samstyles," Lila

explained. "Even if it is a temptation to do so."

"So what should I do if someone asks me about them?" Sam queried.

"Turn the customer over to Erin or me or one of the other salespeople."

"No problem," Sam assured her.

"Great," Lila said. She stuck her hand out, and Sam shook it. "We're glad to have you. I think this is going to work out just fine."

Sam went out front, where Erin was still behind the cash register, and clasped her hands over her head like a boxer who'd just won the heavyweight championship.

"You got it!" Erin called, a delighted look on her face. She quickly came around the counter and gave Sam a hug.

"I got it!" Sam screamed, hugging her back. "I am so happy!"

"Me, too," Erin agreed. "This is going to be great!"

"You're supposed to train me," Sam said.

"Piece of cake," Erin said. "Total piece of cake."

Erin spent the next two hours running Sam through what her duties would be.

Fortunately, it was a quiet morning, so Sam didn't have to stand around too much while Erin waited on customers.

Around noon Erin turned to her. "Got it all?" she asked.

"Yeah," Sam replied. "Sort of. I guess."

Erin grinned. "You'll get the hang of it quick," she said. "I bet you're a natural."

"Right," Sam agreed. *Yeah, right,* she thought dejectedly. *How can I keep it all straight? Cash register, sales tax, restocking, resetting shelves, cleaning the dressing rooms, wiping the counters, marking down sale items, helping customers—*

"Well, here comes your first customer," Erin said as a short, somewhat pear-shaped young woman with frizzy brown hair came into the shop alone.

"You want me to take her?" Sam asked nervously.

"Sure, why not?"

"Because—"

"Go for it!" Erin whispered, and gave Sam a little shove toward the young woman.

*This girl is seriously in need of a makeover!* Sam thought as she went over to the customer. *And she's dressing all wrong for her body type! Actually, she's not all that bad-looking. There's potential. Although you'd never know it right now.*

The girl had on a short, baggy gray summer-weight sweater and very tight yellow pants, which only emphasized the extra twenty pounds around her hips and thighs.

*It's amazing,* Sam thought. *She looked in the mirror this morning and said to herself, "Yes, I look good."*

"May I help you?" Sam asked as she approached the girl.

"Uh, no," the girl said quickly. "I'm just looking."

"Well," Sam asked, since Erin had told her to be persistent, "what did you have in mind?"

The girl dropped her voice. "I'm going to a big singles party tonight in Portland," she whispered self-consciously. "And I want to look drop-dead gorgeous."

"You've come to the right place." Sam smiled. "We've got great clothes here."

"And sexy," the girl added, grabbing Sam's arm. "I want to look really sexy."

"Great!" Sam said. "I'm sure we can find something that will be perfect."

"My husband left me six months ago," the young woman continued. "For his secretary. I caught them together. In our bed."

"Oh, gee . . ." Sam said, at a total loss.

"She's the sex-bomb type," the woman went on. "Now I want to be the sex-bomb type. I need something like . . . like this."

She made her way over to a small rack of fire-engine-red catsuits with zippers up the front.

*Are you kidding?* Sam thought while the woman looked the garment over. *It's the wrong size, the wrong color, and the wrong cut. It will emphasize all your shortcomings and hide all your assets. In other words, a huge fashion disaster.*

"How much is it?" the woman asked Sam.

Sam gulped. "Let's see." She picked up the catsuit and looked for the price tag. "Here it is. It's one hundred forty dollars. Plus tax."

"I'm going to try it on," the woman said happily.

"I'll show you to the dressing room," Sam said, and led the customer to the back of the store, where the dressing rooms were located.

As she'd been trained, Sam sat outside the dressing room until the woman came out. When she did, she flounced over to one of the full-length, three-sided mirrors and gave herself a big spin.

*Oh, God,* Sam thought. *She looks kind of like the red water tower outside my hometown of Junction. Only upside down.*

"This screams sex bomb, don't you think?" the woman asked eagerly. "I love it! How do I look?"

"You know, the sex-bomb look is over-rated," Sam began.

"What does that mean?" the woman asked, studying herself from all angles. She pulled the zipper at the front of the catsuit down lower.

"Well, maybe you're not the . . . the sex-bomb type, exactly," Sam said tentatively.

The woman turned to Sam. "Please tell me the truth. I don't want to make a fool of myself. How do I look?"

"Well . . . you look . . . you could look better," Sam whispered.

"But—"

"Listen," Sam said, "let me pick out something for you."

"But—"

"Let me try," Sam insisted. "If you don't like anything I pick, you can always buy the catsuit. Plus, I think I can get you something at a better price."

The woman shrugged, and Sam hurried back into the main sales area. She made three quick stops, at three different final-sale racks, and came back with a simple black minidress, not too short, with a flared skirt that would hide the woman's hips and thighs, a silk pajama-style outfit in a rich forest green, and a long multicolored gauzy skirt to be worn with a scoop-necked body-suit.

"Try these!" Sam said.

"I don't know. . . ."

"Please. I really do know fashion," Sam insisted.

The woman shrugged again, took the clothes, and went into the changing room. In a couple of minutes she came back out, wearing the forest-green pajama-style out-fit.

She looked at herself in the full-length mirror. "This is gorgeous!"

"I know!" Sam agreed. "It looks so good on you! See how the deep green flatters your complexion? And the flow of the pajama-style bottoms looks great on you!"

"I look thinner, I know I do!" the woman said.

"Absolutely," Sam confirmed. "And much sexier, without going into overkill."

"You're a genius!"

"Thanks!" Sam cried, giddy with happiness. "And here's the best part—it costs half as much as the catsuit!"

"I'll take it!" the woman cried. "You are a complete genius."

"Thanks," Sam said. "Now follow me, and I'll get you rung up out front."

The woman followed Sam to the register, where Erin dutifully totaled her sale and wrapped up her purchase.

"Have fun tonight," Sam said. "You're gonna look incredible!"

The woman gave Sam a huge grin and then happily left the store.

"Have you lost your mind?" Erin asked Sam when the woman was gone.

"What do you mean?" Sam asked her, surprised.

"You just turned a one-hundred-forty-dollar sale into a seventy-dollar sale," Erin exclaimed.

"Well, yes, but—"

"That woman was ready to buy the cat-suit!"

"It made her look like a cow," Sam replied with dignity.

"But she was ready to buy it!" Erin cried. "You would have made more commission."

"It was horrible on her!" Sam defended herself. "She looked like a deformed apple. And she's only been single for six months. She caught her husband—"

"Sam, time out," Erin said. "You're a salesperson here, you're not a fashion cop or a psychologist!"

"So I was supposed to let her walk out of the store looking like crap?" Sam asked, her hands on her hips.

"The customer is always right," Erin reminded her.

"But—"

Erin sighed. "You're lucky Lila didn't see that transaction."

"How come?" Sam asked.

"Because she would have killed you," Erin said.

This time it was Sam's turn to sigh. "I've got a lot to learn, huh?"

"About good taste, no," Erin joked. "About selling clothes for a living, absolutely yes!"

Sam pulled her bicycle into the short driveway at the Flirts's house at about 9:15 that night. She'd worked the entire day at the Cheap Boutique, and had basically been on her feet for nine straight hours.

*I'm whipped,* Sam thought. *Totally whipped. And my feet are killing me!*

Billy and Carrie were hanging out together in the living room when Sam entered. Billy, on the couch, had his guitar out and was playing a couple of new songs for Carrie, who was lying on the floor at his feet.

"Hey, you found a job?" Billy asked when Sam entered the room. "Congrats."

"How'd you know?" Sam asked him.

Carrie pointed to the name tag that Sam was still wearing. It said *Cheap Boutique* in big printed letters and *Sam* in hastily written script.

"Sherlock Sampson," Carrie said.

"Yeah," Sam said to them. "I'm doing my best to correct the fashion missteps of the civilized world."

"How's the money?" Billy asked.

"If I have anything to do with it," Sam said, thinking back to the incident with the pear-shaped woman and the catsuit, "the money is pretty lousy."

"This came for you tonight," Billy said, holding up an envelope with Sam's name on it.

"Really?" Sam asked. "Who's it from?"

"Your former employer," Billy said.

"Dan Jacobs?"

"Not Dan," Carrie informed Sam. "The monsters. They dropped it off earlier."

"How'd they find out I was here so quickly?" Sam wondered out loud.

"Ian told them," Carrie said, shrugging. "With him, word travels fast."

Sam laughed and took the envelope from Billy. Then she kicked off her cowboy boots, went into the kitchen to get herself a glass of milk, and sat down at the kitchen table to read the note.

Dear Sam,

Help! Help help help help help help!
Every day is worse than the one before. Kiki has more or less moved in with Dad—she's basically living here. And she's like some horror movie come to life. Every morning for breakfast she makes us drink alfalfa juice that she makes in a juicer. We don't know what pus tastes like but we are sure that alfalfa juice is worse! Then she bosses us around like we're her slaves. Everything you used to have to do, we have to do. For her! Meanwhile, our dad just sits there and practically drools over her. It is mondo disgusting.

Is there anything we can do so that you can come back to us? Pretty please? We'll be your best friends. We even promise to eat granola every meal. And like it!

Becky and Allie

Each of the twins had scrawled her name, and then made a lip print under it with lipstick.

*Well, well, well,* Sam thought. *The worm is turning. But there's nothing that could make me go back to the Jacobses now. I've got it all under control.*

# TEN

Sam let herself into the Flirts's house after another exhausting day at the Cheap Boutique, and flung herself down on the couch to catch her breath.

*I'm totally exhausted,* she thought, kicking off her cowboy boots. *Again. Three days on the job there, and my feet still feel like they're about to break off. Or as Pres would say, my dawgs are barkin'.*

*A bath,* Sam decided, her eyes lighting up at the prospect. *What I really need is a bath. A really long, hot one.*

"Hel-lo!" Sam called out, too exhausted to get off the couch.

No one answered.

"Cool," Sam said with a sigh, "home alone."

She padded upstairs into the bathroom and turned the water on in the old claw-foot porcelain tub. She moved the old-fashioned handles around until she got the temperature just where she wanted it to be. She poured in some French bath oil that Erin had given her. And then, to top it all off, she added some bubble bath.

*Ahhhh. In about five minutes, I'll be in heaven,* Sam thought. *Now the question is, do I have a copy of the latest Hollywood gossip rag to read in the tub?*

Just then the phone rang. Sam hurried downstairs—the upstairs extension wasn't working—to answer it.

"Flirts," she said into the phone. "Bridges talkin'."

The voice at the other end of the line laughed. "Cresswell talkin'," Emma said, imitating Sam.

"Hi," Sam said, wiggling her toes to relieve some of the ache.

"I just wanted to see if you were home."

"I'm home. *Finally,*" Sam said, settling

down on the couch for a few moments to talk with her friend.

"Katie's been asleep ninety minutes and she's already had three nightmares," Emma reported. "I could stand talking to someone who's not a kid."

"My job is a nightmare," Sam quipped.

"Really?" Emma asked. "I thought you'd love selling clothes."

"I do," Sam said. "I've got a real knack for it."

"So?"

"A knack for convincing people not to buy stuff that makes them look like dog meat," Sam explained. "You would be amazed at what bad taste a lot of girls have. What am I supposed to do, let them think they look good when they don't?"

"Well, they should appreciate that. What's the problem?"

Sam put her legs up on the couch. "The problem is that my boss wants me to tell them they look fabulous in everything. Have you ever seen two hundred pounds in stretch velvet? It's not a pretty sight."

"But if you're really helping them and

they're buying clothes anyway, why would your boss object?" Emma asked.

"Because the most trendy, most expensive stuff just doesn't look that good on that many people," Sam explained. "I seem to have this gift for finding great-looking stuff on sale—probably because I do it for myself all the time."

"How's the perfume doing?" Emma asked. The Cheap Boutique was one of the very first outlets they'd selected for Sunset Magic perfume. Emma and Carrie had decided that if the perfume sold well there, they were going to try to market it later in the summer in various places around the state of Maine.

"Sunset Magic? Unbelievable today!" Sam chortled. "The whole shipment that came in is already sold out."

"That's twenty-four bottles!" Emma exclaimed happily.

"Gone," Sam repeated. "History. Out of the store."

"I'll bring you more tomorrow," Emma said. "We've got plenty in storage."

"Whatever," Sam said. "I'm a walking ad. I wear it every day."

"Thanks, Sam," Emma said gratefully.

"Hey, I'm a bud," Sam replied philosophically, getting more comfortable on the couch. She reached down to massage her still-aching feet.

"So how's life with Pres?" Emma asked her, changing the subject.

"You mean how is it living in the same house? It's totally cool."

"I'm glad!"

"I told you it would work out fine," Sam said breezily. "And yes, Miss Ice Princess, I'm not even getting near his room at night."

"So everything is perfect. That's great!"

"Well, close to perfect . . ." Sam said slowly.

"Which means?"

"Oh, just that there might have been only one Coke left in the fridge yesterday," Sam said, trying for a touch of humor.

"So?"

"And it just might have been Billy's," Sam continued lightly, "and I just might have drunk it."

"Well, that doesn't sound so awful," Emma said with a laugh.

147

Sam swung her legs back down to the floor. "Yeah," she agreed, "except the same thing happened the day before yesterday."

"Buy more Coke," Emma counseled.

"And toilet paper," Sam said significantly.

"Toilet paper?"

"Girls use more than guys do," Sam said. "It's, like, biological."

"Sam," Emma asked, "did you use up all the toilet paper?"

"Only once," Sam answered. "This morning. First thing this morning."

Emma groaned. "One more problem and Billy's going to be really irritated. I wouldn't imagine he'd be especially easygoing."

"Oh, Billy's no problem," Sam joked, "as long as you don't strand him in the bathroom in the morning without toilet paper." Sam winced at the recollection.

"Oops," Emma said.

"Yeah, no kidding," Sam agreed. "But it's not my fault! I never had to remember to buy things like toilet paper before!"

"Didn't you do the shopping at the Jacobses?"

"Well, yeah, but I bought, like, an entire case at a time, so we never ran out. Anyway, enough about me. What's going on with you and your mom?"

A week or so earlier, Emma had gotten into a terrible fight with her mother, Katerina Cresswell. Kat had come to the island by surprise, had seen that Emma was back with her old boyfriend, Kurt Ackerman, and had basically had a complete fit.

And not only was she mad, she put her money where her mouth was.

*Actually,* Sam thought, *she put Emma's money where her mouth is. Or took Emma's money away from her mouth. Or something like that. In any case, she cut Emma off financially. Emma even had to ask the Hewitts for a raise!*

"The same," Emma reported. "Meaning I am still cut off from the family millions unless I give up Kurt."

"That is so beat," Sam said. "She hasn't given in?"

"Not yet," Emma commented. "I'm not holding my breath, either."

"Drag," Sam commented as she listened to the sound of rain beginning to come down on the roof of the house.

"I'll survive," Emma said. "Somehow."

"I didn't know it was supposed to rain," Sam commented on the apparent change in the weather.

"Sam, it's perfectly nice out," Emma said.

"I can hear it raining," Sam challenged.

"That's weird," Emma said, "because I can see the moon right from my bedroom window."

"I guess it's one of those really local storms or— Oh, my God!"

"Sam, what is it?" Emma cried.

But Sam had already slammed the phone down and taken off like a rocket up the stairs.

The slippery stairs. Which were covered in water, with a pool at the landing.

It was too late. Far too late. When Sam opened the bathroom door, the bathtub had long since overflowed—there were at least two inches of water, and another inch of bubbles, on the bathroom floor.

Instantly Sam turned off the water going into the tub.

The silence was deafening . . . except for the gurgle of water escaping through the cracks, and dripping out to who knew where.

"Oh, my God," Sam said again, even though there was no one in the bathroom, or even the house, to hear her. "My life is over."

"So, Sam," Billy said, "I think we've got a little bit of a problem here."

Sam looked to Pres, who was sitting to her left, for help. She didn't get any.

"I'll say," Sam agreed. "You need to get a more modern bathtub. One with one of those automatic things that drain it when the water gets too high."

"That's not funny," Billy said.

"Yeah, it kinda was," Pres said, grinning.

Sam threw him a grateful look.

"Okay," Billy relented. "It was funny. But we've still got a problem here."

It was now midnight. Billy and Pres had gotten home from a recording session they were doing in Portland, and when Billy had seen the damage from Sam's flood in the bathroom, he'd gone momentarily ballistic.

*And he didn't even see the worst of it,* Sam thought. *Because I had about two hours to clean up before they got home! I hope no one's planning on taking a shower anytime soon. There isn't a dry towel in the whole house.*

"I'll pay for the damage," Sam offered meekly.

"Do you have any idea how much that will be?" Billy asked.

"No," Sam admitted.

"Let's see," Billy said, picking up a pencil that was on the table. "Floorboards buckled, water damage on walls, water damage on floor, rugs ruined, wiring affected—"

Sam gulped. "I get the picture," she said.

"Good," Billy said, chewing on the pencil.

"I think the insurance should cover it," Pres suggested.

"True," Billy said. Sam breathed a sigh of relief. There was a lot of damage.

"Of course," Pres drawled, "our landlord's gonna pitch a fit."

"Get him to buy you a new bathtub," Sam suggested.

"Sam," Pres said softly, "I don't know how to tell you this, but—"

"Let me tell her," Billy said sharply. "It really was my decision."

"You want me out," Sam said matter-of-factly. "I get the picture."

"It's nothing personal," Billy assured her. "This just isn't working out."

Sam took a deep breath. One part of her wanted to cry out that this really wasn't her fault—it wasn't her fault that the house was an antique wreck and that the bathtub was from the Stone Age. And another part of her knew it *was* her fault, that they had been doing her a favor and she had really messed up.

Just then Sam recalled the lyrics of a song that Pres had once sung to her about knowing when to hold 'em and knowing when to fold 'em.

"Okay," she said. "I'm outta here. And I'm really sorry for the trouble."

A look of respect passed over Billy's face. Clearly he wasn't used to Sam actually taking responsibility for her actions.

"Thanks, Sam," he said. "I'll just try to forget that this little problem ever happened."

"What problem?" Sam asked innocently. All three of them laughed.

"It musta been a sight," Pres drawled,

153

"that water pourin' down the stairs like water over a busted dam."

"It was a riot," Sam assured him.

"Glad I missed it," Billy said, an ironic tone in his voice. "Anyway, you can stay a few days, until you find another place to live."

"Thanks," Sam said sincerely. "That's really nice of you."

*And just where the hell am I going to find another place to live?* she thought desperately. *I'll be camping out on the beach soon. How did everything turn into such a nightmare?*

"Carrie says that Allie and Becky really want you to come home," Billy said.

"It ain't home anymore!" Sam joked.

"Would you?" Pres asked her.

"It's not up to the monsters," Sam said. "It's up to Dan the Man Jacobs. He hasn't asked me."

"Maybe he'll change his mind," Billy suggested.

"I doubt it," Sam said. "He's too mesmerized by Kiki."

"Maybe she'll change her mind, then," Pres said.

"And maybe Diana will join a nunnery," Sam quipped, "'cuz that's just about how likely it is. Well, not to worry. You guys know me—I always land on my feet!"

"Good attitude," Billy approved.

"Sure," Sam said easily. *I am so screwed,* she said in her mind. *I am so totally screwed.* She stood up and stretched nonchalantly. "Anyway, I'm going into the kitchen."

"So?" Pres asked.

"Anybody want a glass of . . . *water?*" Sam asked, barely getting the word out without cracking up.

Billy answered by throwing the pencil he was holding at her. Sam neatly caught the pencil in her left hand, stuck it behind her ear, and sauntered away.

*Never let 'em see you sweat.*

# ELEVEN

"Oh, God, that feels so heavenly," Sam groaned as Pres massaged the aching instep of her foot with vanilla-scented massage oil. "I'll give you three hours to stop."

"Standin' on your feet all day is really getting to ya, huh?" Pres said, reaching for some more oil.

It was the next evening, and Pres and Sam were the only ones home. Billy had gone to the movies with Carrie.

"Maybe it's the cowboy boots," Sam said, sighing with pleasure as Pres started on the ball of her right foot.

"So wear something else on your feet," Pres suggested.

"Please," Sam said, "I have an image to maintain."

"Sell anything today?"

"Three outfits that were on sale," Sam admitted. "And I talked one girl out of buying this fake-fur minidress we just got in—it would have been a four-hundred-dollar sale!"

"Dang, why'd you do that?" Pres exclaimed.

"Because she looked like a dead polar bear that didn't have the sense to lie down!" Sam exclaimed. "How could I let her walk out of the store like that? What if she went around telling people that I said she looked good? My rep is at stake!"

"Yeah, but your job might be at stake, too," Pres reminded her. "Switch feet."

Sam put her left foot on Pres's lap. "I know I should keep my mouth shut," Sam moaned, "but I just can't help it! Erin sells four times as much stuff as I do! It's not that she lies to them or anything, but she's just really diplomatic."

"Something you have never been," Pres said with a chuckle.

"I calls 'em like I sees 'em," Sam

drawled. "Mmmmmm, I can't even tell you how good this feels."

"You want a back rub, too?" Pres offered.

"What is this, be-nice-to-Sam day?"

"You complainin'?"

"Heck, no," Sam said, sitting up so she could turn over. "This is bliss!"

Pres poured some more oil on his hands and reached under Sam's white cotton T-shirt. She wasn't wearing a bra.

"Wherever I move you have to promise to come over every night and do this until I fall asleep," Sam groaned. "Where did you learn to give such a great massage?"

"Oh, this cute girl back in Nashville taught me," Pres said. "She used to massage my—"

"Hey!" Sam objected, raising her head to look back at Pres.

"I'm teasing you," Pres said with a laugh.

"I knew that," Sam replied with dignity.

She closed her eyes again as Pres's strong fingers began to knead the tired muscles at the back of her waist, then traveled up her spine.

"So, you got any leads on a place to live?" Pres asked her.

"Not yet, but I will," Sam said.

"Maybe you ought to go talk with Dan Jacobs," Pres suggested.

"Not on your life," Sam said firmly.

"But he offered to let you live there," Pres reminded her. "And as you've discovered, it's really tough to find an affordable place on the island in the middle of the summer season."

"I'm resourceful," Sam said. "I'll think of something."

Pres reached for the massage oil. "Like what?" he pressed.

"Like I don't know, okay?" Sam asked, rolling over. "Why do I suddenly feel myself getting all tensed up again?"

"You do, huh?" Pres asked.

"I do. Look, I appreciate your concern, but I'm gonna take care of it," Sam insisted.

"Okay."

"Okay." She stared up at him. "I still feel tense."

"Well, that's a danged shame," Pres drawled. "Maybe this will help." He leaned down and kissed her softly. "How's that?"

"Interesting," Sam mused.

Pres leaned over again. "How about this?" He kissed her more fully, until she wrapped her arms around his neck and pulled him down on top of her.

They kissed for a long time, until Sam felt weak and breathless. Her T-shirt was up around her neck and Pres's shirt was unbuttoned.

"You want to go to my room?" Pres asked huskily.

"Yes. No."

Pres groaned and threw himself off Sam.

"I'm sorry!" Sam exclaimed. "I'm just . . . I don't know what I am."

"Sam, you're nineteen years old."

"That's a fact," Sam mumbled.

"We're in your basic long-term committed relationship."

"I know," Sam replied.

"So?"

"That doesn't mean I have to be ready to make love, does it?" Sam asked.

Pres lay on his back and stared at the ceiling. "No, it doesn't."

"Just because I love to kiss you and hold you doesn't mean I have to—"

"I know, I know," Pres said. He turned to

her and shook his head ruefully. "There's only one thing I can say. No, make that two things."

"What's that?"

"One is I need a cold shower," Pres said. "And two is it's a danged good thing that you're moving out!"

Four hours later Sam lay on the couch in the living room, unable to sleep. Billy had come home, and he and Pres had already gone to sleep. But Sam was still tossing and turning on the lumpy couch.

*Where am I gonna find a place to live?* she worried. *Maybe there really isn't anyplace. I refuse to go groveling to Dan Jacobs. And I don't have a clue what other options I have. Maybe I just need to throw in the towel and leave the island.*

*Leave the island.* The thought filled Sam with dread.

"And go where?" she whispered out loud in the dark. "Not Kansas. Not if my life depended on it!"

And then another thought struck her—a good one—and she sat up quickly. "Susan," she said.

162

Susan was Susan Briarly, Sam's biological mother. Sam had found out only recently that she was adopted—her parents had never told her the truth. Sam had been devastated by the news for a long time—in fact, it was still hard for her to deal with—but she had managed to track down her biological mother, and they had become friends. She'd even met her biological father, who was Israeli.

*And I'm Jewish,* Sam recalled, *or at least my biological parents are. It still seems like the weirdest thing in the world. Someday I'm gonna learn more about that religion, I really am* . . .

"Gotta call Susan," Sam muttered. She got up, turned on the light, rooted around in her purse for her little address book, and finally located Susan's number in Oakland, California. Then she dialed the long-distance number.

*It's three hours earlier there,* Sam thought while she listened to the phone ring. *I hope Susan is still up* . . .

"Hello?"

"Susan! It's Sam!"

"Sam! Oh, I'm so glad to hear from you!" Susan replied. "How are you?"

"Really good!" Sam said. "Well, kind of good."

"What's wrong?" Susan asked quickly. "Are you sick?"

"No, no, nothing like that," Sam assured her. Then she quickly explained what had happened with her au pair job, and how she had no place to live. "So, I'm kind of . . . uh . . . adrift, I guess you could say," Sam concluded lightly.

"Poor Sam!" Susan said. "You've had a terrible time!"

"Yeah, it's been your basic nightmare," Sam agreed. "And it's next to impossible to find an affordable place to live on this island in the middle of the summer."

"It's a very upscale place, I know," Susan said. "Is there anything I could do to help?"

Sam took a deep breath. "Maybe. I . . . I was wondering if . . . depending on what happens, maybe I could come to California."

"Come here?" Susan asked hesitantly.

"I guess you don't want me, huh?" Sam asked, gulping back her disappointment.

"Oh, it's not that at all!" Susan cried. "It's . . . well, it's Carson. We're kind of having a hard time right now."

Carson was Susan's husband. He and Sam didn't get along at all.

"I'm sorry," Sam said quickly. "I guess it isn't a good idea."

"Hold on, hold on," Susan said. "Maybe I have a better one. I've got a friend in San Francisco, an actress, who just separated from her husband. She's got a little boy and she's desperate to find a good au pair right away."

"Hey, that's me!" Sam exclaimed.

"That's just what I was thinking!" Susan agreed. "Should I call her for you and make sure the job is open?"

"That would be fantastic!" Sam cried. "Oh, my God, that means I'd be moving to California!"

"Well, I'm just selfish enough to tell you it would make me really happy," Susan said softly. "I'll call her as soon as I can, okay?"

"Okay," Sam agreed. "And I'll call you in a few days. Wow, this is fantastic!"

"Sam?"

"Uh-huh?"

"I can't wait to see you," Susan said warmly. "I think California has your name on it."

"Thanks, Susan," Sam said.

They said good-bye, and Sam hung up the phone and lay back down on the couch. *It means good-bye Emma, good-bye Carrie, and good-bye Pres,* Sam thought. *It means the end of my life on Sunset Island. But maybe it could be the beginning of something really wonderful. . . .*

But the tears that fell from her eyes told a different story.

# TWELVE

*What's this?* Sam thought as she stood behind the counter at the Cheap Boutique the next day and tried to see who was coming into the shop.

Two girls were trying to maneuver their way into the entrance of the store; both of them appeared to be hooked up to intravenous tubes. But a rack of dresses was in between Sam and the door, so she couldn't make out their identity.

"Poor kids," Erin Kane said, coming out from behind the counter to go help them.

"Yeah," Sam agreed.

"Both of them must be sick," Erin commented.

"Probably just out of the hospital," Sam said. "Maybe even on a pass from the hospital or something."

"Drag," Erin said as she tried to open the door for the girls. She pushed once, and then twice.

"It's gonna be hard for them to try on clothes," Sam muttered, straightening a display of jewelry. She sighed and moved a rhinestone Elvis pin to the front of the display. *I am so miserable,* she thought. *I suppose I should be happy, but I'm not. I don't want to go to California—at least not now, not permanently. But it's either that or Kansas, and Kansas is not a choice I'll make in this lifetime.*

*At least I won't mind giving up this job,* Sam thought with a sign. *Lila's got me working, like, sixty hours this week. I see Pres 'cuz I'm still at his house, but I hardly ever get to see Emma and Carrie.*

Sam looked up. Erin was still working on getting the door open for the girls, but the door to the boutique opened out, and one of the girls had somehow gotten her IV pole wedged in the doorway.

Finally Erin got the door open, and the two girls came into the shop.

For the first time Sam saw who it was: Becky and Allie Jacobs.

Both of them were wearing hospital scrubs—Becky's were blue, and Allie's were green. And both had huge, ugly-looking bandages on their arms where the IV needles were inserted.

Erin disappeared for a minute into the back of the store, even as Allie and Becky came over and surrounded Sam.

"Oh, my God," Sam cried, "what happened to you guys? Are you okay?"

"We're weak," Allie whispered.

"Depleted," Becky sighed as she wheeled her IV slowly toward Sam.

"On our last legs," Allie muttered.

"Suffering," Becky put in.

"Dying," Allie moaned.

"What happened?" Sam cried. "Were you guys in an accident? This is so horrible!"

"We're on strike," Becky told her.

"Hungry strike," Allie said.

"*Hunger* strike," Becky corrected.

"Whatever," Allie said. "I'm hungry. Starved."

"It's supposed to do that, you idiot," Becky said.

"You're the idiot," Allie said accusingly.

"You!" Becky yelled.

"You!"

"Hold on," Sam said. "Are you guys sick or not?"

The twins ignored her.

"Whaddaya mean?" Becky asked her sister.

"You thought of this!" Allie accused.

"It's a good idea," Becky said, defending herself.

"Can't we, like, go for a burger?" Allie asked.

"As soon as we get out of here," Becky said. "Play Café, here we come!"

"Not there," Allie said. "What if someone we know sees us?"

"Hold on!" Sam demanded. She took a quick look around the store to see if there were any customers she was neglecting. There weren't. Then she said a quick thank-you that her boss wasn't around, either.

"Okay, let me get this straight," Sam told the twins. "You're on a hunger strike?" *How can you be on a hunger strike if you're going to the Play Café?* she added to herself.

"Hungry strike," Allie muttered, glaring at Becky.

"We demand change," Becky explained.

"Right away," Allie added.

"Instantly. Like yesterday," Becky said.

"Is this some political thing?" Sam asked, remembering the previous summer, when Allie had been in one of her weirder phases. That time, she'd hacked off all her hair because she wanted to be a nun.

"No," Becky said, wheeling her IV around the floor slowly. She stopped in front of some shirts and picked one up. "How do you think this would look on me?"

"Like cold crap on a stale bagel," Allie told her sister.

"You're such a snot, Becky."

"Two people in this store are crazy and I am not one of them!" Sam screamed. "Now what is going on? And why are you hooked up to IVs?"

Allie and Becky looked at each other. And then they cracked up.

"Props," Becky cried with glee.

"They're fake," Allie agreed. "We added

them for dramatic effect. The needle isn't really in our arms or anything. We rented these things!"

"Pretty dramatic, huh?" Becky asked.

"Hey!" Sam scolded. "What do you think you're doing, scaring everybody like that? Erin and I both thought you were sick, and that you just got out of the—"

Allie choked back her laughter. "Chill, Sam," she said.

"We're doing it for you!" Becky hastened to explain.

"For me?" Sam asked. "What are you talking about?"

It was Erin who figured it out.

"Sam," Erin finally said, "your former kids are giving their dad a lesson in power politics."

"Granola politics," Becky said, and grinned.

"You mean—"

"Yup," Allie said. She went on to explain how she and Becky had gotten together earlier in the week and decided to take matters into their own hands about their dad, Kiki Coors, and Sam.

Since the previous Thursday, the girls

hadn't eaten anything except granola. In fact, they were demanding it for breakfast, lunch, and dinner.

"It's driving Kiki nuts," Becky confided.

"We want her out," Allie said. "Bad."

"And we need you back, Sam," Becky said, a pleading look in her eyes. "We can't take it anymore. Every day is awful."

"Amen," Allie agreed.

*They want me to come back? And be their au pair again?* Sam thought. *That means I wouldn't have to move to California! It would certainly solve my housing problem. And save my relationship with Pres, which would be pretty tough to handle long distance. It would even save my feet—they're still killing me.*

"You can't turn us down!" Allie cried. "Look how pathetic we are!"

"Yeah!" Becky agreed. "Do you realize we just took the bus over here attached to these things? Us! On public transportation!"

"Looking like this!" Allie added. "That proves how desperate we are!"

Sam looked over at the pleading faces of the twins. *Well, Pres once told me that sometimes the devil you know is better than the devil you don't know . . . but Dan and Kiki would probably never go for it. And I shouldn't let the twins off so easy, either.*

"What makes you think your father would agree?" Sam asked, folding her arms.

"Oh, believe me, he'd agree," Allie assured her. "How do you think it would look to have his daughters starve to death?"

"Yeah, he'll get arrested or something!" Becky added.

"Well," Sam said slowly, as if she were perfectly confident, "what if I don't want to come back? I've got a great job here—"

"And a great discount on clothes," Erin added.

"Right," Sam agreed. *And no place to live,* she added in her mind, *but I'm not about to tell them that.*

Becky and Allie looked at each other.

"We've thought about that," Becky said finally.

"We're prepared to make it worth your while," Allie said solemnly.

"Oh, yeah?" Sam asked. "This'd better be good. And make it quick. I'm on duty here."

Allie and Becky looked at each other

again. Then Allie reached into the pocket of her scrubs, took out a folded piece of paper, and handed it slowly to Sam.

Sam opened it and started to read. It was printed in capital letters.

### PEACE TREATY

WHEREAS ALLIE JACOBS AND BECKY JACOBS, BEING OF SOUND MIND AND SOUND BODY, REALIZE THAT THEY ARE NOW SWIMMING IN DEEP DOO-DOO AT HOME, THEY HEREBY PETITION SAMANTHA ("SAM") BRIDGES AS FOLLOWS . . .

\*　　\*　　\*

"Sam!" Dan Jacobs cried when he saw it was Sam who was at the door. "Come in, come in."

"Thanks, Dan," Sam said lightly as she stepped into the familiar confines of the Jacobses' front hallway.

"So," Dan said, "to what do we owe this visit?"

"Oh, nothing," Sam said cheerfully. "I was biking in the neighborhood, and I thought I'd stop in."

"I'm glad you did," Dan replied. "You want coffee?"

"That'd be great," Sam agreed, following Dan as he headed into the kitchen.

It was the next day, Thursday, around six in the evening. Allie and Becky had tipped Sam off the day before that Kiki Coors would be visiting her parents in Portsmouth, New Hampshire, and that their dad would be home right around six.

So, according to the plan they'd made, Sam made it her business to drop in on the Jacobs family around dinnertime. The twins had promised they would be upstairs playing Nintendo.

Dan poured Sam a glass of iced coffee, and another one for himself.

"So," he said, smiling broadly at her, "I'm glad you decided to let bygones be bygones."

"That's why they call them bygones," Sam said brightly, stirring some sugar into her coffee and smiling her most winning smile back at Dan.

"So . . . Allie and Becky say you're working at the Cheap Boutique," Dan said.

"It's a great job," Sam said. "I love it!"

"You're doing well?" Dan asked, taking a sip of his coffee.

"Real well," Sam assured him. "Really, really well."

"That's good," Dan said, his enthusiasm sounding a little forced.

Sam continued, "I'm a natural at selling clothes."

"Yes, you do have a great sense of, um, fashion," Dan said, nodding. "I remember how much you helped the girls. Yep . . . well, like I said, I thought you always were great with the twins," Dan went on after a pause.

"Yeah," Sam agreed, "I was, wasn't I? Hey! tell 'em to come down and say hello!"

Dan shook his head. "I wanted to talk to you about them."

Sam took a slow, deliberate sip of coffee. Then she looked up. "What about?" she asked innocently.

"Well . . . they're not doing so well," Dan confessed, nervously stirring his coffee, the ice cubes clinking.

"No!" Sam said, feigning great concern.

"Yes!" Dan confided.

"It must be a phase," Sam commented,

suppressing a smile. "Whatever it is, they'll get over it." She looked at her watch. "Gee, Dan," she said, getting up from the table, "it's been really good seeing you, but—"

"Sam, please stay a minute," Dan said, getting up and putting his hand on Sam's arm.

"Yes, Dan?" She sat back down at the table.

"Thanks," Dan said gratefully. "Can I get you some more coffee?"

Sam shook her head. "I'm kind of hungry, though," she mused mischievously.

"A muffin!" Dan cried, jumping up. He got a muffin, put it on a plate, and put it down in front of Sam. "We've got muffins just going to waste because the girls . . ." He stirred his coffee some more. "They're on a hunger strike," he said finally, in a low voice.

"Really?" Sam said, arranging her features in a surprised expression.

"Really," Dan assured her.

"Drag," Sam said, taking a bite of the muffin. "So they're not eating at all?"

"Oh, they're eating . . ."

"Eating? But they're on a hunger strike," Sam said, seemingly baffled.

*This is the most fun I've ever had!* she thought gleefully, but she was careful to keep her face totally neutral. *It serves you right for firing me for no good reason, Dan Jacobs!*

"They're not eating," Dan continued, "except for granola."

"Granola?" Sam asked, sounding surprised. "Weird, because that's what they were eating the morning—"

"Exactly," Dan said meaningfully. "That's exactly it."

"What's it?"

"They're eating granola because they want you back!" Dan said, practically shouting.

"No!" Sam said.

"Yes!" Dan cried, putting his head in his hands. "I can't believe it myself. And I was a total idiot. I should never have let you go."

"Gee, Dan," Sam said, swallowing the last of her muffin, "I don't know what to say."

"Would you . . . could you . . . would

you consider coming back and working for us again?" Dan asked quickly, the words tumbling out one on top of the other.

"That's a really nice offer," Sam said, "but I've already got a job. A great job, as I said."

"I was afraid you'd say that," Dan said sadly. He got up from the table and walked to the bottom of the stairs. "Becky? Allie? There's someone here to see you!"

"Who is it?" Sam heard Becky yell.

"Sam!" Dan called back.

"Sam? Sam Bridges? Saaaaaam!" Becky and Allie cried simultaneously. They came running down the stairs so fast that they nearly crashed, and headed toward Sam with open arms.

*Oh, God, they're going to hug me,* Sam thought.

But Becky and Allie ran right past Sam and on into the kitchen, where they started cramming their mouths with apples, bananas, grapes, and other fruit from a bowl that was on the kitchen counter. Then they threw open the cupboard, pulled out the chips, and tore into the bag.

"Sam's here," Becky mumbled as she stuffed her face with grapes. "We can eat."

"Yum," Allie mumbled around a huge mouthful of chips. "Bring on the burgers! Gimme some fries! I'm dying for junk food!"

"Pizza!" Becky yelled. "Let's order pizza!"

Dan turned to Sam and made a pleading gesture with his hands. "Please, Sam, are you sure there's nothing I can do to persuade you to come back?"

"What about Kiki?" Sam asked innocently.

At the sound of the name Kiki, Becky and Allie fell on the floor and squirmed around convulsively.

"Fit!" Becky yelled, flailing around.

"Gag me! Gag me!" Allie screamed.

"Girls, stop that," Dan said sharply. He turned back to Sam. "Let me worry about Kiki. Now, are you sure there's nothing I can do?"

"Well," Sam said, smiling her most angelic smile, "maybe there is something. . . ."

"Really?" Dan asked hopefully.

"Maybe," Sam said.

"Give her anything, Dad," Becky said. "Please!"

"Where's the phone number of the pizza place?" Allie asked.

"Sam?" Dan asked.

"How about if we all go into the living room to talk?" Sam suggested.

"Great!" Dan said with relief.

"Don't say 'great' yet," Sam cautioned with an evil grin. "You haven't heard my demands yet. Not by a long shot."

# THIRTEEN

"Are you glad to be back with the twins?" Carrie asked, dipping a french fry in some ketchup.

"I'm glad to have a place to live," Sam admitted. She reached for her second burger. "Happiness always makes me ravenous."

It was the next day, and that morning Sam had moved back into the Jacobses' house. *Back into my own room,* Sam had thought as she rolled around blissfully on the bed. *My own bathroom, my own desk, my own mess. Bliss!*

The twins were at camp, and Sam had arranged to meet Carrie and Emma on the boardwalk for lunch.

"That granola strike they pulled off was truly amazing," Emma said with a laugh. She leaned her head back so the afternoon sun beat down on her face.

"Ingenious," Sam agreed.

"So what did Dan do about Kiki?" Carrie asked.

"Oh, I think he put his manly foot down or something," Sam said. "Actually, I bet she was totally sick of the twins. Let's face it, they can be a pain in the butt."

"And now they're your pain in the butt again," Emma reminded her. "Did you mind quitting the Cheap Boutique?"

Sam grabbed the last french fry and stuffed it into her mouth. "Not a bit. I'd much rather buy clothes than sell them. Frankly, I was a terrible salesperson. I think Lila was ready to fire me anyway. Hey, I'm still hungry. Let's walk down the boardwalk to the soft-serve ice cream place."

They tossed their garbage in a nearby trash can and strolled down the board-walk.

Sam threw her arms open wide and twirled around in a circle. "I love this place!" she cried.

"Someone put something funny in her burger," Carrie told Emma.

"You know what really impressed me, Sam?" Emma said as they walked along. "How well you handled everything that happened to you. You weren't even stressed out."

"Well, you know me," Sam said, "I'm the coolest."

"No, you're not," Carrie said, pulling her sunglasses out of her purse.

"One of the coolest?" Sam tried.

"What would you have done, for example, if Dan Jacobs hadn't rehired you?" Carrie asked. "I was really, truly ready to beg Graham and Claudia to put you up for the rest of the summer!"

"Wow, you should have done it!" Sam exclaimed. "I could be living in the lap of luxury at the home of a famous rock star instead of slaving for the twins!"

"Seriously," Emma said, "what would you have done?"

Sam pushed her hair out of her face. "Okay, I have a confession to make," she finally said. "I was scared. I mean really, really scared." She walked over to the

185

railing and leaned against it. Emma and Carrie followed her.

"Why didn't you tell us?" Emma asked.

"If you don't know by now that you can be honest with us . . ." Carrie began.

"So I'm a slow learner," Sam said. She stared out at the ocean. "At first I really thought everything would be okay. But then nothing was okay. Everything kept going wrong, you know?"

"Yeah, we do," Emma said softly.

"I started thinking . . . it's really tough to be a grown-up." Sam made a face. "God, is that what I am? A grown-up?"

"I'd never accuse you of that," Carrie teased.

"Grown-ups are, like, dull and boring," Sam said. "I don't want to be one of those!"

"Some people are dull and boring no matter what age they are," Emma said.

Sam twirled a lock of her hair around one finger. "It's funny . . . I couldn't wait to get out of Kansas so I could be on my own and have an actual life. But I found out something this week. Being on your own can be pretty scary."

Emma and Carrie nodded in agreement.

"I got so worried," Sam said. "And I didn't know what to do. So finally I called Susan in California—"

"Your birth mother?" Emma interrupted.

Sam nodded. "I told her what happened. And she told me her friend in San Francisco needed an au pair. So . . . I was going to move to California. . . ."

"And you didn't even tell us?" Carrie exclaimed.

"I would have," Sam insisted. "It's not like I wanted to leave, but I just didn't know what else to do! I called Susan back, though, as soon as I'd finished talking to Dan Jacobs."

"Don't you know we would have found a way for you to stay on the island?" Emma asked.

"How?" Sam demanded. "You don't have any money anymore. No one had a place for me to live—and I certainly had no intentions of going back home to Kansas."

"Sam, we would have raised the money, or scoured this entire island, but no way would we have let you leave," Carrie said earnestly.

"Really?" Sam asked, a lump coming to her throat.

"Don't you know how much we love you?" Emma asked softly.

Sam gulped hard. "I guess it would be hard for the Flirts to find a backup singer as perfect as I am," she said, trying to be funny.

"It's not about the band," Carrie said. "It's about friendship. And family."

"Sometimes family is who you choose," Emma added softly. "And we choose you."

"Thanks," Sam said, trying hard not to cry. "Just . . . thanks." She took a deep breath. "Well, enough mush. Let's race to the ice cream place!"

Sam took off first, sprinting fast, Emma and Carrie behind her. But right before she got to the ice cream place, she stopped dead in her tracks. Right in front of her was the Soak the Sap booth. Once again Iron Eagle was there by himself, doing absolutely no business. An old Doors tune blasted out of his stereo.

"Hi, there," Sam said, walking over to him.

"Hey, babe," Iron said. "Want your old job back?"

"Gee, no," Sam said. "But I'd like to try and soak the sap."

"No sap," Iron said.

"You," Sam said, pointing at him.

"Me?"

Sam nodded. At that moment Emma and Carrie came up next to her. "My former employer," she told them.

"Either of you babes need a job?" Iron asked. "It pays commission."

Emma and Carrie shook their heads.

"Too bad," Iron said.

Sam reached into her pocket and pulled out a twenty-dollar bill. She waved it at Iron. "Does this suggest anything to you?"

Iron looked at the money. "You want me to be the sap, huh?"

"That's about the size of it," Sam agreed.

Iron scratched his chin. "I haven't had any customers all day," he said, still eyeing the money. Finally he took it. "Okay, babe, you're on. You can't dunk me, anyway."

Iron put the money into his pocket, then he climbed the ladder into position. "Okay, press the button to start the tires swinging, honey pie. Then give it your best shot."

"Wait just a minute," Sam called to him. "I have to do your job first." She cleared her throat. "Ladies and gentlemen!" she called loudly. "Come on over here and play soak the sap! Get the guy in the ugly tie-dye wet, get him all wet, get him soaking wet!"

Emma and Carrie began to laugh.

"Don't be shy!" Sam yelled in her best barker style. "It's soak the sap, he's the sap and you can soak him!" Sam turned to her friends. "Why, I believe I'll take a shot!" she drawled, in her best imitation of Lorell. Then she picked up a football, took a step back, and heaved it at the tire.

A direct hit!

Iron Eagle fell into the water and came up sputtering, his gray hair plastered to his head.

Emma and Carrie jumped up and down and applauded, as did the small crowd that had gathered.

"Hey, you were standing way too close!" Iron thundered, pushing the dripping hair off his face. "You cheated!"

"Sucks, doesn't it?" Sam said with a big grin. "See ya around, *honey pie!*"

"That was great!" Carrie exclaimed.

"And worth every penny of that twenty dollars," Sam added as she walked up to the ice cream booth.

After they all got their cones, they strolled back down the boardwalk.

"So, do you think the twins will act any differently now that they've got you back?" Carrie asked, licking at her vanilla cone.

"They have to," Sam said, slurping her chocolate ice cream. "They put it in a contract. Plus, I basically blackmailed Dan."

"What did you do?" Emma asked.

"Well, the twins promised to make their own breakfast every morning for the rest of the summer—"

"No granola, is my guess!" Carrie put in.

"And they have to make coffee in the morning and hand me my first cup when I come downstairs!"

"You think they'll do it?" Carrie asked.

"They'd better," Sam replied smugly.

"And how did you blackmail Dan?" Carrie wondered.

"I made him give me a twenty-five-dollar-a-week raise!" Sam cried gleefully. "And Saturday nights off! Or else I walk!"

"No!" Emma said, stunned.

"I really did!" Sam said. "Now, am I a genius, or what?"

Emma shook her head. "I have to hand it to you, Sam, you're a genius."

"Have you ever considered law school?" Carrie asked. "Because you are one tough negotiator!"

"I am, aren't I?" Sam agreed, a huge grin spreading across her face. "I really am!"

When Sam got back to the Jacobses' she brought in the mail and looked through it as she walked into the house. Her kitten, Bubba, rubbed up against her legs.

"I was always gonna come back for you," she told the kitten. "I wouldn't have deserted you permanently."

Since none of the mail was for her, she put it on the kitchen table and went up to her room.

*My room,* Sam thought with a sigh of satisfaction. *I love the way that sounds.*

On her dresser, she noticed something that she had somehow missed before. It was a letter addressed to her. She sat on her bed and quickly opened it.

Dear Sam,

I guess you know that we're really glad you're back. We know sometimes we've been mean to you and stuff, but we didn't really appreciate you until you weren't here anymore. But then we got to thinking about our mom and how she just left us, like she didn't care about us at all. And then we thought about you and how you wanted to stay, even though you aren't really related to us or anything. So what we want to say is that we kind of think of you as part of our family now. We figure family can be anyone you love, right?

Love,
Becky and Allie

P.S. We will try not to be such monsters but there are no guarantees.

Sam felt tears in her eyes as she put the letter down. *It's funny,* she thought. *It's almost the exact same thing Carrie and Emma told me. Maybe family really can be anyone you love. And maybe deep down inside I do love the twins a little.*

*Not a lot. A little.*

And with one last look at the room she loved in the house she loved on the island she adored, Sam bopped back downstairs to forage for junk food.

Some things never change.

# SUNSET ISLAND MAILBOX

Dear Readers,

Okay, here we are, off and flying into another summer of absolutely amazing books. I hope you loved both Sunset Love and Sunset Fling. And I hope you're going to love Sunset Tears and Sunset Spirit, both coming later this summer.

Then there's another Sunset book coming out right before Christmas, called Sunset Holiday. So you can see that there's a lot of great reading coming up.

As I write this, Jeff and I are in the middle of rehearsals for my new play, Anne Frank & Me. The world premiere is here in Nashville later this year, and we're both excited and a little nervous. The good news is that we've assembled another amazing cast of mostly teenage actors who are going to be really, really great.

Many of you have sent in requests that I try to work subjects into the series, such as date rape and teen pregnancy. I appreciate these suggestions, and am anxious to hear more. And here's my question for you: What's the dumbest advice that any grown-up ever gave you?

If any of you are coming to Nashville, be sure to send me a letter before your trip. And you know the drill about fan mail . . . you send me a letter, it gets answered personally.

*See you on the island!*
*Best-*
*Cherie Bennett*

Cherie Bennett
c/o General Licensing Company
24 West 25th Street
New York, New York 10010

All letters printed become property of the publisher.

*Dear Cherie,*
*You are one of my favorite authors for one reason. You always write back to your readers. I know many authors are busy but you take the time to do so. You are such a kind, caring person. Do you ever get stumped thinking of* Sunset *titles?*

*Fondly,*
*Caron Edwards*
*Tacoma, WA*

Dear Caron,

A lot of readers ask me about what I do in my spare time, and I always tell them "answer my fan mail!" So far, I haven't gotten stumped thinking of titles, and I've had lists and lists of possibilities sent to me by helpful fans like you!

> Best,
> Cherie

*Dear Cherie,*

*I would like to start by saying that I am one of (if not the) biggest fan of your writing. I have gotten my best friend Robyn hooked, too. We actually read parts of your books over the phone. And, to my surprise, I found my name on the back cover of* Sunset Sensation. *That's right, my name is Erin Kane!*

> *Love always,*
> *Erin Kane*
> *Newington, CT*

Dear Erin,

Your letter made our day! Jeff read the return address and said "You're not gonna believe who this letter is from, Cherie." And he was right. Hey, are you and your Sunset sisters interested in hearing me read from some of the Sunset books? Because maybe we can do some books-on-tape!

> Best,
> Cherie

*Dear Cherie,*

*Hey—as we say in Tennessee—and hi—as we say in California. I live in Tennessee, but I'm from California. My friend Angela Tims got me reading your great, cool, fun, and entrancing books. One question: why does Sam call Emma the "Ice Princess"? Please keep writing more great books.*

> *California Tennessee girl,*
> *Shawna Sorley*
> *Ripley, TN*

Dear Shawna,

Well, you and I both know how cool Tennessee is! All fan letters get forwarded from New York to me here in Nashville. When you get all caught up on your Sunset books, you'll see that Sam calls Emma the "Ice Princess" because she looks like she'll never sweat! But wait 'til you see what happens later this summer. . . .

> Best,
> Cherie